A COMPLETING OF

For Filip, Laura and Charlie – the planets, stars and heavenly bodies in my solar system

&

For Jane Austen – I hope we meet some day

ROSE   JANE
SERVITOVA   AUSTEN

A COMPLETING OF

The Watsons

Warm Wishes,

Rose Servitova

WOOSTER PUBLISHING

First published in 2019 by
Wooster Publishing
Limerick
Ireland

Paperback	ISBN: 978 1 78846 115 3
eBook – mobi format	ISBN: 978 1 78846 116 0
eBook – ePub format	ISBN: 978 1 78846 117 7
Amazon paperback	ISBN: 978 1 78846 118 4

Produced by Kazoo Independent Publishing Services
222 Beech Park, Lucan, Co. Dublin
www.kazoopublishing.com

Kazoo Independent Publishing Services is not the publisher of this work. All rights and responsibilities pertaining to this work remain with Wooster Publishing.

Kazoo offers independent authors a full range of publishing services. For further details visit www.kazoopublishing.com

Cover design by Andrew Brown
Printed in the EU

She had not known the weight until she felt the freedom.

— The Scarlet Letter, NATHANIEL HAWTHORNE

PREFACE

In September 2017, I found myself on a flight to Bath to attend the city's annual Jane Austen festival. My debut novel, *The Longbourn Letters*, was more widely celebrated than I'd anticipated or was prepared for. I was also voluntarily curating a six-month long Austen bicentenary celebration, as well as working full-time and raising a husband, a three-year-old and a six-year-old. I was exhausted.

Novice that I was, I felt pressure to quickly produce another book in order to maximise the exposure I had received from my debut. Thus began my efforts with the adventures of Captain McCarthan – a kind of Bertie-Wooster-on-a-horse tale of foolishness, comedy and luck. The story, however, wasn't working. I had struggled with it for weeks and as I sat on that flight to Bath, I had the lightbulb moment as to how I could fix it – the horse needed dialogue! It was at that moment I realised that my marbles were officially lost and perhaps it would be best if I stepped away from Captain McCarthan and his horse.

Immersing myself in Jane Austen's life in Bath was exactly what I needed. I walked in slow motion, hugging trees that might have been around in Austen's time, placing my feet ever so mindfully on the cobbles she must have walked on and indulging in my obsession for forty-eight hours. Relaxed, rejuvenated and reconnected with Austen, I sat cheerfully on the flight home and decided that I would park Captain McCarthan and his talking horse and, instead, embrace my craziness and permit myself to have the audacity to finish one of Austen's incomplete works, *The Watsons*.

Austen wrote only a handful of chapters of *The Watsons* before leaving it aside, never to return to finish it. As we know, Austen reworked and rewrote her manuscripts several times, with the greatest attention, before sending them off for publication – she had not got far with *The Watsons*. Virginia Woolf wrote of this scant fragment, "the stiffness and bareness of the first chapters" suggest that "she was one of those writers who lay their facts out rather baldly in the first version and then go back and back and back and cover them with flesh and atmosphere." The responsibility for me, therefore, was to remain loyal to Austen's original story and yet to place extra colour while creating a plot typical and worthy of Austen with which to see it to its conclusion.

Some experts claim that Austen abandoned *The Watsons*, which she started in Bath in 1803, as the story was too close to her own. In *The Watsons*, four unmarried sisters live with their ill and poor clergyman father, facing a life of dependence on the goodwill and charity of extended family if he dies and they have not married. Such insecurity and vulnerability were preoccupations in Austen's own life. In a case of life imitating art, Austen's clergyman father, George Austen, died soon after, leaving a wife and two daughters seeking cheap living arrangements in Bath – their standards sinking with every move of home they were forced to make. They had become financially dependent on Jane's brothers (who had their own large families also to provide for) but who saw them finally settle, permanently, at Chawton Cottage, Hampshire.

There exists an account of Jane Austen's plans for *The Watsons*. Austen's nephew James Edward Austen-Leigh claimed in his *A Memoir of Jane Austen*, some sixty-seven years after *The Watsons* was written, that Jane Austen's sister Cassandra told her nieces that Jane had told her (a little) of what she had envisioned for the plot. They later told him and he then wrote about it many decades later. However, when I let it stew and percolate within my grey cells, I was not convinced that, had she returned to it, she would have followed these intentions to the letter. For the most part, I stuck with Austen-Leigh's claim, but one particular point was absolutely contrary to Austen's style elsewhere and I just could not convince myself that if she had come back to the manuscript, she would have progressed it in that way. In the end, I decided to remain loyal to Austen's style rather than to go with the other claim.

Finally, the two principal characters in *The Watsons* reflect aspects of Austen as I see her based on her letters and several biographies of her life – namely her humour and vivacity as well as her vulnerability and concerns. I have included in this novel a few lines from her letters which demonstrate her genius for wit.

My hope is that every reader enjoys this version of *The Watsons*.

Rose Servitova

CHAPTER ONE

The first winter assembly in the town of Dorking in Surrey was to be held on Tuesday, October 13th and it was generally expected to be a very good one. A long list of county families was confidently run over as sure of attending and sanguine hopes were entertained that the Osbornes themselves would be there.

The Edwardses' invitation to the Watsons followed, of course. The Edwards were people of fortune, who lived in the town and kept their coach. The Watsons inhabited a village about three miles distant, were poor and had no close carriage, and ever since there had been balls in the place, the former were accustomed to invite the latter to dress, dine and sleep at their house on every monthly return throughout the winter.

On the present occasion, as only two of Mr Watson's children were at home, and one was always necessary as companion to himself, for he was sickly and had lost his wife, one only could profit by the kindness of their friends. Miss Emma Watson, who was very recently returned to her family from the care of an aunt who had brought her up, was to make her first public appearance in the neighbourhood.

Her eldest sister, Elizabeth, whose delight in a ball was not lessened by ten years' enjoyment, had some merit in cheerfully undertaking to drive her and all her finery to Dorking on the important morning.

As they splashed along the dirty lane, nestled together in the old chair, Emma was eager to learn more about her dear siblings, the friendliness of neighbours and the likelihood of agreeable gentlemen attending the ball. Elizabeth, wishing to oblige, delighted in the opportunity to instruct and caution her inexperienced sister.

"I dare say it will be a very good ball and among so many officers you will hardly want for partners. You will find Mrs Edwards' maid very willing to help you with your hair but whatever you do, do not permit her to place flowers in it. I made this error once and appeared as the Hanging Gardens of Babylon for the evening. It is almost winter now so you should be safe. I would advise you to ask Mary Edwards' opinion if you are at all at a loss for she has very good taste. If Mr Edwards does not lose his money at cards, you will stay as late as you can wish for; if he does, he will hurry you home perhaps, but you are sure of some comfortable soup."

Emma nodded to indicate she was taking note of Elizabeth's advice.

"I hope you will be in good looks. I should not be surprised if you were to be thought one of the prettiest girls in the room. There is a great deal in novelty. Perhaps Tom Musgrave may take notice of you but I would advise you by all means not to give him any encouragement. He needs very little and generally pays attention to every new girl. He is a great flirt, however, and never means anything serious."

"I think I have heard you speak of him before," said Emma. "Who is he?"

"A remarkably agreeable young man of good fortune, a universal favourite wherever he goes, first and foremost with himself and then with any young ladies present. Most of the girls hereabout are in love with him, or have been. I believe I am the only one among the ladies to have escaped with a whole heart and yet I was the first Mr Musgrave paid attention to when he came into this country six years ago. Very great attention did he pay me too but he never captured my heart."

"And how came yours to be the only cold one?" said Emma, smiling.

"There was a reason for that," replied Elizabeth, changing colour. "I have not been very well used among them, Emma. I hope you will have better luck."

"Dear sister, I beg your pardon if I have unthinkingly given you pain."

"When first we knew Tom Musgrave," continued Elizabeth, "I was very much attached to a young man of the name of Purvis, a particular friend of Robert's, who used to be with us a great deal. Everybody thought it would have been a match."

Emma, unsure how best to respond, remained silent but her sister after a short pause went on:

"You will naturally ask why it did not take place and why he is married to another woman, while I am still single. But you must ask her, not me; you must ask your sister Penelope. Yes, Emma, Penelope was at the bottom of it all. She thinks everything fair for a husband. I trusted her. She set him against me, with a view to gaining him herself and it ended in his discontinuing his visits and soon after marrying somebody else. Penelope makes light of her conduct but I think her treachery very bad. I shall never love any man as I loved Purvis but that is not to say that I shall never love any man. I hope I shall, for I must. But Tom Musgrave – why, he should not be mentioned with Purvis in the same day!"

They rode on for a few minutes in near silence, Elizabeth occasionally pointing out some feature in the landscape and enquiring of Emma if she remembered it. The concern which Emma felt in relation to the previous discussion, however, meant that she must return to it and with furrowed brow she began,

"You quite shock me by what you say of Penelope," said Emma. "Could a sister do such a thing? Rivalry, treachery between sisters! I shall be afraid of being acquainted with her. But I hope it was not so. Appearances were against her, I am sure. Loyalty and unselfishness is what I think when I think of family; those happy beliefs keeping me warm all these years. A family may be crossed by circumstance or by others but not by each other. There is no stronger bond."

"You do not know Penelope. There is nothing she would not do to get married. Do not trust her with any secrets of your own. I never shall again. She has her good qualities but she has no faith, no honour, no scruples where she can promote her own advantage. How surprised you look, Emma. I do not wish to alarm you and yet I wish with all my heart that she was well married. I declare I had rather have her well married than myself."

"Than yourself! Yes, I can suppose so. A heart wounded like yours can have little inclination for matrimony."

"Not much indeed, but you know we must marry. I could do very well single for my own part – a little company, a pleasant ball and a glass of mead every now and then would be enough for me. But our father cannot provide for us and I dread relying on the good humour and fortunes of our brothers. No, we must marry, if at all possible, for it is very bad to grow old and be poor and laughed at."

Their father's old mare, Lady Macbeth, clanked and clanged along the bad road, instinctively avoiding all the worst parts. The girls were, therefore, thrown about less often than they might have been by a more ambitious horse.

"Not that I can ever quite forgive Penelope, but for all her meddling in other people's affairs, she has had her own troubles," continued Elizabeth. "She was sadly disappointed in Tom Musgrave, who afterwards transferred his attentions from me to her and of whom she was very fond, but he never means anything serious. When he had trifled with her long enough, he began to slight her for Margaret and poor Penelope was very wretched. I am glad you were not with us then for she screamed and scolded dawn till dusk."

Emma's spirits continued to sink at such contrary domestic scenes to those she had long imagined. Elizabeth continued,

"And since then Penelope has been trying to make some match at Chichester. She won't tell us with whom but I believe it is a rich old Dr Harding, uncle to a Miss Shaw she goes to see. She has taken a vast deal of trouble about him. When she went away the other day, she said it should be the last time and said it with such a look that I could not help but feel sorry for poor Dr Harding. His fate is sealed, whether he is aware of it or not. I suppose you did not know what her particular business was at Chichester, nor guess at the object which could take her away from Stanton to Miss Shaw's just as you were coming home after so many years' absence."

"No indeed, I had not the smallest suspicion of it. I considered her engagement to Miss Shaw, just at that time, as very unfortunate for me. I had hoped to find all my sisters at home – and would have assumed that they would have been unless something of a very urgent nature took them away – to be able to make an immediate friend of each."

"Perhaps in her eyes it was very urgent, for I suspect the doctor to have had an attack of asthma and that she was hurried away on that account. It would never do to lose a husband before he had become one. The Shaws are quite on her side – at least, I believe so, but she tells me nothing. She professes to keep her own counsel."

"I am sorry for her anxieties," said Emma, "but I do not like her plans or her opinions. I shall be afraid of her. She must have too bold a temper. To be so bent on marriage, to pursue a man merely for the sake of situation, is the sort of thing that shocks me. I cannot understand it. Poverty is a great evil but to a woman of education and feeling it ought not, it cannot, be the greatest. I would rather be teacher at a school (and I can think of nothing worse) than marry a man I did not like. Anything is to be preferred or endured rather than marrying without affection."

"I would rather do anything than be teacher at a school," her sister said, laughing. "I have been at school, Emma, and know what a life they lead. You never have. I should not like marrying a disagreeable man any more than yourself but I do not think there are many very disagreeable men. I think I could like any good-humoured man with a comfortable income. The more comfortable his income, the more good-humoured I shall find him. I suppose our aunt brought you up to be rather refined."

Elizabeth smiled while Emma, eager to defend her upbringing, said, "Indeed I do not know. My conduct must tell you how I have been brought up. I am no judge of it myself. I cannot compare my aunt's method with any other person's because I know no other. She raised me as she judged best. Perhaps I am a little reserved from want of company."

"But I can see in a great many things that you are very refined," continued Elizabeth. "I have observed it ever since you came home and I am afraid it will not be for your happiness. Penelope will laugh at you very much."

"*That* will not be for my happiness, I am sure. If my opinions are wrong, I must correct them. If they are above my situation, I must endeavour to conceal them but I doubt whether ridicule ... Has Penelope much wit?"

"Yes. She has great spirits, or rather cunning."

"Margaret is more gentle, I imagine?"

"Yes, especially in company. She is all gentleness and mildness when anybody is by but she is fretful and irritable among ourselves. She loves gossip. It is what she lives for.

Poor creature! She is possessed with the notion of Tom Musgrave's being more seriously in love with her than he ever was with anybody else and is always expecting him to come to the point. This is the second time within this twelvemonth that she has gone to spend a month with Robert and Jane on purpose to encourage him by her absence. I am sure she is mistaken and that he will no more follow her to Croydon now than he did last March. He will never marry unless he can marry somebody very great – Miss Osborne, perhaps, or something in that style."

"Your account of this Tom Musgrave, Elizabeth, gives me very little inclination for his acquaintance."

"You are afraid of him. I do not wonder at you."

"Not afraid, indeed. I dislike him."

"Dislike Tom Musgrave! No, that you never can. I defy you not to be delighted with him if he takes notice of you. I hope he will dance with you and I dare say he will, unless the Osbornes come with a large party and then he will not speak to anybody else."

"He seems to have most engaging manners!" said Emma. "Well, we shall see how irresistible Mr Tom Musgrave and I find each other. I suppose I shall know him as soon as I enter the ball-room. He must carry some of his charm in his face."

"You will not find him in the ball-room, I can tell you. You will go early, that Mrs Edwards may get a good place by the fire, and he never comes till late. If the Osbornes are coming, he will wait in the passage and come in with them."

"Then I shall be surprised if he notices me at all."

"I should like to look in upon you, Emma, for I believe

it will be a marvellous ball and the neighbourhood, for not having had one for months, will be inclined to find it excellent. If it was only a good day with my father, I would wrap myself up as soon as I had made tea for him and James should drive me over so I should be with you by the time the dancing began."

"What! Would you come late at night in this chair?"

"To be sure I would. There, I said you were very refined and that's an instance of it. I care not a jot in what fashion I appear."

Elizabeth laughed again and Emma, for a moment, made no answer, then at last she said, "I wish, Elizabeth, you had not made a point of my going to this ball. I wish you were going instead of me. Your pleasure would be greater than mine. Your laughter more deserved. I am a stranger here and know nobody but the Edwardses. My enjoyment, therefore, must be very doubtful. Yours, among all your acquaintance, would be certain. It is not too late to change. Very little apology could be requisite to the Edwardses, who must be more glad of your company than of mine, and I should most readily return to my father and should not be at all afraid to drive this quiet old creature home. Your clothes I would undertake to find means of sending to you."

"My dearest Emma," cried Elizabeth, warmly, "do you think I would do such a thing? Not for the universe! But I shall never forget your good nature in proposing it. You must have a sweet temper indeed! I never met with anything like it! What a fine thing to learn, at last, that I have a sister without trick or self-interest. And would you really give up the ball that I might be able to go to it?

Believe me, Emma, I am not so selfish as that comes to.
No, though I am nine years older than you are, I would not
be the means of keeping you from being seen. You are very
pretty and it would be very hard that you should not have as
fair a chance as we have all had to make your fortune. No,
Emma, whoever stays at home this winter, it shan't be you.
I am sure I should never have forgiven the person who kept
me from a ball at the age of nineteen."

Emma expressed her gratitude and Elizabeth put her
arm around her and gave a short and fond squeeze.

"The next turning will bring us to the turnpike. You may
see the church-tower over the hedge and the White Hart is
close by it."

Such were the last sounds of Elizabeth's voice, before
they passed through the turnpike-gate and entered on
the pitching of the town, the jumbling and noise of which
made further conversation most thoroughly undesirable.
Old Lady Macbeth trotted heavily on, wanting no direction
of the reins to take the right turning and making only
one blunder, in proposing to stop at the milliner's, before
moving on towards the correct row of houses. Mr Edwards
lived in the best house in the street and the best in the
place, if Mr Tomlinson, the banker, might be indulged in
calling his house at the end of the town, with a shrubbery
and sweep, in the country.

CHAPTER TWO

As they approached it, Emma could see that Mr Edwards' house was higher than most of its neighbours, with four windows on each side of the door, the windows guarded by posts and chains and the door approached by a flight of stone steps.

"We have almost arrived," said Elizabeth, "and by the market clock, we have been only thirty minutes coming, which is quite a wonder when one considers Lady Macbeth's reluctance to move at all. Is it not a nice town? The Edwardses have a noble house, you see, and they live quite in style. The door will be opened by a man in livery, with a powdered head, I can tell you. But before I forget, you will take notice of who Mary Edwards dances with?"

"I will remember her partners, if I can, but you know they will be all strangers to me."

"Only observe whether she dances with Captain Hunter more than once. I have my fears in that quarter. Not that her father or mother like officers but if she does, you know, it is all over with poor Sam. And I have promised to write him word who she dances with."

"Is Sam attached to Miss Edwards?"

"Did not you know *that*?"

"How should I know it? How should I know in Shropshire what is passing of that nature with my brother in Surrey from the scanty communication which passed between you and me?"

"I am sorry, dear Emma, that I did not tell you. I hardly know what I write and whether it would be of any interest to you, so far away. It would be just like me to send accounts of Nanny's new boots than your brother being in love. Since you have been at home, I have been so busy with my poor father and our great wash that I have had no leisure to tell you anything but, indeed, I concluded you knew it all. Sam has been very much in love with her these two years and it is a great disappointment to him that he cannot always get away to our balls. Mr Curtis won't often spare him and just now it is a sickly time at Guildford."

"Do you suppose Miss Edwards inclined to like him?"

"I am afraid not. You know she is an only child and will have at least ten thousand pounds."

"But still she may like our brother."

"Oh, no! The Edwardses look much higher. Her father and mother would never consent to it. Sam is only a surgeon, you know. Sometimes I think she does like him. But Mary Edwards is rather reserved and I cannot tell for sure."

"Unless Sam feels on sure grounds with the lady herself, it seems a pity to me that he should be encouraged to think of her at all."

"A young man must think of somebody," said Elizabeth, "and why should not he be as lucky as Robert, who has got a good wife and six thousand pounds?"

"We must not all expect to be individually lucky," replied Emma. "The luck of one member of a family is luck to all."

"Mine is all to come, I am sure," said Elizabeth. "I have been unlucky enough and I say that you have not fared much better with our aunt marrying again so foolishly. But let us dwell on better things," said Elizabeth, as the carriage ceased moving. "You will have a good ball, I dare say. I shall long to know what you think of Tom Musgrave."

Emma had seen the Edwardses only briefly one morning at Stanton. They were, therefore, all but strangers to her and though her spirits were by no means insensible to the expected joys of the evening, she felt a little uncomfortable in the thought of all that was to precede them. Her conversation with Elizabeth, too, had given her some very unpleasant feelings with respect to her own family and of the kind of gentlemen she might expect to meet that evening. She was half-afraid to learn much more and found her tongue become quietened and her conduct more closed.

There was nothing in the manner of Mrs or Miss Edwards to give immediate change to these ideas. The mother, though a very friendly woman, had a reserved air, the type which would become open and intimate on greater acquaintance but in early encounters would demonstrate a great deal of formal civility. The daughter, a genteel-looking girl of twenty-two, with her hair in papers, seemed very naturally to have caught something of the style of her mother. Emma was soon left to know what they could be, by Elizabeth's being obliged to hurry away, and some very languid remarks on the probable brilliancy of the ball were all that broke, at intervals, a silence of half an hour, before they were joined by the master of the house. Mr Edwards had a much easier and more communicative air than the ladies of the family. He was fresh from the street and he came ready to tell whatever might interest. After a cordial reception of Emma, he turned to his daughter with,

"Well, Mary, I bring you good news. The Osbornes will certainly be at the ball tonight. Horses for two carriages are ordered from the White Hart to be at Osborne Castle by nine."

"I am glad of it," observed Mrs Edwards, "because their coming gives a credit to our assembly. The Osbornes being known to have been at the first ball will dispose a great many people to attend the second. It is more than they deserve, for in fact they add nothing to the pleasure of the evening. They come so late and go so early, but great people have always their charm."

Mr Edwards proceeded to relate every other little article of news which his morning's lounge had supplied him with. They chatted with greater briskness, till Mrs Edwards' moment for dressing arrived and the young ladies were carefully recommended to lose no time. Emma was shown to a very comfortable apartment and as soon as Mrs Edwards' civilities could leave her to herself, the happy occupation, the first bliss of a ball, began. The girls, dressing in some measure together, grew unavoidably better acquainted. Emma found in Miss Edwards the show of good sense, a modest unpretending mind and a great wish of obliging. When they returned to the parlour where Mrs Edwards was sitting, respectably attired in one of the two satin gowns which went through the winter and a new cap from the milliner's, they entered it with much easier feelings and more natural smiles than they had taken away. Their dress was now to be examined. Mrs Edwards acknowledged herself too old-fashioned to approve of every modern extravagance, however sanctioned, and though complacently viewing her daughter's good looks, would give but a qualified admiration. Mr Edwards, not less satisfied with Mary, paid some compliments of good-humoured gallantry to Emma at her expense. The discussion led to more intimate remarks and Miss Edwards gently asked Emma if she were not often reckoned very like her youngest brother. Emma thought she could perceive a faint blush accompany the question and there seemed something still more suspicious in the manner in which Mr Edwards took up the subject.

"You are paying Miss Emma no great compliment, I think, Mary," said he, hastily. "Mr Sam Watson is a very good sort of young man and I dare say a very clever surgeon, but his complexion has been rather too much exposed to all weathers to make a likeness to him very flattering." Mary apologised, in some confusion.

She had not thought a strong likeness at all incompatible with very different degrees of beauty. There might be resemblance in countenance and the complexion even if the features were very unlike.

"I know nothing of my brother's beauty," said Emma, "for I have not seen him since childhood, but my father reckons us alike."

"Mr Watson!" cried Mr Edwards. "Well, you astonish me. There is not the least likeness in the world. Your brother's eyes are grey, yours are brown. He has a long face and a wide mouth. My dear, do you perceive the least resemblance?"

Mrs Edwards was quick to agree. "Not the least. Miss Emma Watson puts me very much in mind of her eldest sister and sometimes I see a look of Miss Penelope and once or twice there has been a glance of Mr Robert, but I cannot perceive any likeness to Mr Samuel."

"I see the likeness between her and Miss Watson," replied Mr Edwards, "very strongly, but I am not sensible of the others. I do not much think she is like any of the family but Miss Watson, but I am very sure there is no resemblance between her and Sam. None in the slightest."

This matter was settled and they went to dinner.

"Your father, Miss Emma, is one of my oldest friends," said Mr Edwards as he helped her to wine when they were drawn round the fire to enjoy their dessert. "We must drink to his better health. It is a great concern to me, I assure you, that he should be such an invalid. I know nobody who likes a game of cards, in a social way, better than he does and very few people that play a fairer rubber. It is a thousand pities that he should be so deprived of the pleasure. For now we have a quiet little Whist Club that meets three times a week at the White Hart, and if he could but have his health, how much he would enjoy it! There is nothing, I believe, that gets between a keen card-player and his cards, except his own decline."

"I dare say he would join you, sir, and I wish, with all my heart, he were equal to it."

"Your club would be better fitted for an invalid," said Mrs Edwards, "if you did not keep it up so late."

This was an old grievance.

"So late, my dear! What are you talking of?" cried the husband, with sturdy pleasantry. "We are always at home before midnight. They would laugh at Osborne Castle to hear you call that late. They are but rising from dinner at midnight."

"That is nothing to the purpose," retorted the lady, calmly. "The Osbornes and their dismissal of daylight are to be no rule for us. You had better meet every night for cards and break up two hours sooner."

So far the subject was very often carried but Mr and Mrs Edwards were so wise as never to pass that point and Mr Edwards now turned to something else. He had lived long enough in the idleness of a town to become a little of a gossip and having some anxiety to know more of the circumstances of his young guest than had yet reached him, he began with,

"I think, Miss Emma, I remember your aunt very well, about thirty years ago. I am pretty sure I danced with her in the old rooms at Bath, the year before I married. She was a very fine woman then but like other people, I suppose, she is grown somewhat older since that time. I hope she is likely to be happy in her second choice."

"I hope so. I believe so, sir," said Emma, in some agitation.

"Mr Turner had not been dead a great while, I think?"

"About two years, sir."

"I forget what her name is now."

"O'Brien."

"Irish! Ah, I remember, and she is gone to settle in

Ireland. I do wonder that you should not wish to go with her into that country, Miss Watson, but it must be a great deprivation to her, poor lady, after bringing you up like a child of her own."

"I was not so ungrateful, sir," said Emma, warmly, "as to wish to be anywhere but with her. It did not suit them. It did not suit Captain O'Brien that I should be of the party."

"Captain!" repeated Mrs Edwards. "The gentleman is in the army then?"

"Yes, ma'am."

"Aye, there is nothing like your officers for captivating the ladies, young or old. There is no resisting a cockade, my dear."

"I hope there is," said Mrs Edwards, gravely, with a quick glance at her daughter. Emma had just recovered from her own perturbation in time to see a blush on Miss Edwards' cheek and in remembering what Elizabeth had said of Captain Hunter, to wonder and waver between his influence and her brother's.

"Elderly ladies should be careful how they make a second choice," observed Mr Edwards.

"Carefulness and discretion should not be confined to elderly ladies or to a second choice," added his wife. "They are quite as necessary to young ladies in their first."

"Rather more so, my dear," replied he, "because young ladies are likely to feel the effects of it longer. When an old lady plays the fool, it is not in the course of nature that she should suffer from it many years."

Emma fidgeted with her handkerchief and turned her face away. Perceiving this, Mrs Edwards changed the subject to one of less anxiety to all.

With nothing to do but to expect the hour of setting off, the afternoon was long to the two young ladies and though Miss Edwards was rather discomposed at the very early hour which her mother always fixed for going, that early hour itself was watched for with some eagerness.

The entrance of the tea-things at seven o'clock was some relief and luckily Mr and Mrs Edwards always drank a dish extraordinary and ate an additional muffin when they were going to sit up late, which lengthened the ceremony almost to the wished-for moment.

CHAPTER THREE

At a little before eight, the Tomlinsons' carriage was heard to go by – which was the signal for Mrs Edwards to order hers to the door. In a very few minutes the party was transported from the quiet and warmth of a snug parlour to the bustle, noise and draughts of air of the broad entrance passage of an inn. Mrs Edwards carefully guarded her own dress, while attending with yet greater solicitude to the proper security of her young charges' shoulders and throats. She then led the way up the wide staircase, while no sound of a ball but the first scrape of one violin blessed the ears of her followers. Miss Edwards, on hazarding the anxious inquiry of whether there were many people come yet, was told by the waiter, as she knew she would be, that "The Tomlinson family are in the room."

In passing along a short gallery to the assembly-room, brilliant in lights before them, they were accosted by a young man in a morning-dress and boots, who was standing in the doorway of a bedchamber, apparently on purpose to see them go by.

"Ah! Mrs Edwards, how do you do? How do you do, Miss Edwards?" he cried, with an easy air. "You are determined to be in good time, I see, as usual. The candles are but this moment lit."

"I like to get a good seat by the fire, you know, Mr Musgrave," replied Mrs Edwards.

"I am this moment going to dress," said he. "I am waiting for my stupid fellow. We shall have a famous ball. The Osbornes are certainly coming – you may depend upon that, for I was with Lord Osborne this morning."

The party passed on. Mrs Edwards' satin gown swept along the clean floor of the ball-room to the fireplace at the upper end, where one party only were formally seated, while three or four officers were lounging together, passing in and out from the adjoining card-room. As soon as they were all duly placed again, Emma, in the low whisper which became the solemn scene, said to Miss Edwards, "The gentleman we passed in the passage was Mr Musgrave, then. He is reckoned remarkably agreeable, I understand?"

Miss Edwards answered, "Yes; he is much liked by many people but we are not very intimate."

"He is rich, is he not?"

"He has about eight or nine hundred pounds a year, I believe. He is now about nine and twenty years but came into possession of it when he was much younger and my father and mother think it has given him rather an unsettled turn. He is no favourite with them."

"And who is that gentleman over there, calling after the master of the inn?"

"That is Mr Solomon Tomlinson, son of Mr Tomlinson, the banker. He is curate at Wickstead which is attached to

Osborne Castle," replied Mary Edwards, enjoying her role as descriptor of characters. "You will be introduced to him if he happens this way but I do rather hope he does not … or rather that we are too busy dancing … well, what I mean is, there is sufficient time to meet him. I do not wish to be unkind but he does have a lengthiness of speech that does not permit one to be at all sociable. Before he gets to the point, the evening has ended and so few have been danced with."

Emma laughed along with Miss Edwards at this report and marvelled that her companion possessed more humour and less reserve than she had given her credit for.

"I have been caught on too many occasions. Our families are old friends and I am very often obliged to notice him when I had rather not. I am sure he has his charms," she continued, "but I have yet to discover them."

The cold and empty appearance of the room and the demure air of the small cluster of females at one end of it began soon to give way. The inspiriting sound of other carriages was heard and continual accessions of portly chaperons and strings of smartly dressed girls were received, with now and then a fresh gentleman straggler, who, if not enough in love to station himself near any fair creature, seemed glad to escape into the card-room.

Among the increasing number of military men, one now made his way to Miss Edwards with an air of empressement which decidedly said to her companion, "I am Captain Hunter." Emma, who could not help but watch Miss Edwards at such a moment, saw her looking rather distressed but by no means displeased and heard an engagement formed for the first two dances, which made her think her brother Sam's a hopeless case.

Emma in the meanwhile was not unobserved or unadmired herself. A new face, and a very pretty one, could not be slighted. Her name was whispered from one party to another and no sooner had the signal been given by the orchestra's striking up of a favourite air, which seemed to call the young to their duty and people the centre of the room, than she found herself engaged to dance with a brother officer, introduced by Captain Hunter.

Emma Watson was not more than middle height, well made and plump, with an air of healthy vigour which complemented a girl of nineteen years. Her skin was very brown, clear, smooth and glowing, which, with large, lively and often playful eyes, a sweet smile and an open countenance, gave beauty to attract and expression to make that beauty improve on acquaintance. Having no reason to be dissatisfied with her partner, the evening began very pleasantly to her and her feelings perfectly coincided with the reiterated observation of others, that it was an excellent ball.

The two first dances were not quite over when the returning sound of carriages after a long interruption called general notice and "The Osbornes are coming! The Osbornes are coming!" was repeated round the room. After some minutes of increased bustle without and watchful curiosity within, the important party, preceded by the attentive master of the inn to open a door which was never shut, made their appearance. They consisted of, Miss Edwards informed Emma by pointing each out,

Lady Osborne; her son, Lord Osborne; her daughter, Miss Osborne; Mr Howard, formerly tutor to Lord Osborne, now clergyman of Wickstead, the parish in which the castle stood; Mrs Blake, a widowed sister who lived with Mr Howard; her eldest son, a fine boy of ten years old; and Mr Tom Musgrave, who Emma imagined had been imprisoned within his own room listening in bitter impatience to the sound of the music for the last half hour.

In the party's progress up the room, they paused almost immediately behind Emma to receive the compliments of some acquaintance and she heard Lady Osborne observe that they had made a point of coming early for the gratification of Mrs Blake's little boy, who was uncommonly fond of dancing. Emma looked at them all as they passed but chiefly and with most interest on Tom Musgrave, who was certainly a genteel, good-looking young man. Of the females, Lady Osborne had by much the finest person; though nearly fifty, she was very handsome and had all the poise and dignity of rank.

Lord Osborne was a very fine young man of twenty-three years – though long of throat and short of hair. There was an air of awkwardness and restlessness about him, which seemed to speak him out of place in a ball-room. Mrs Edwards had earlier informed Emma that he came to the ball only because it was judged expedient for him to please the borough. He was not fond of women's company and he never danced, she'd said. His domain was the outdoors; everything within four walls made him uneasy. The tall man Emma observed, surrounded by an animated group but looking over their heads at the clock already, appeared to confirm this opinion of him.

Emma then turned her gaze on Mr Howard, who was an agreeable-looking man, a little more than thirty.

At the conclusion of the two dances, Emma found herself, she knew not how, seated among the Osborne set and she was immediately struck with the fine countenance and animated gestures of the little boy, as he was standing before his mother, wondering when they should begin.

"You will not be surprised at Charles's impatience," said Mrs Blake, a lively, pleasant-looking little woman of five or six and thirty, to a lady who was standing near her, "when you know what a partner he is to have. Miss Osborne has been so very kind as to promise to dance her first two dances with him."

"Oh, yes! We have been engaged this week," cried the boy, "and we are to dance down every couple."

On the other side of Emma, Miss Osborne, Miss Tomlinson and a party of young men were standing engaged in very lively consultation. Soon afterwards she saw the smartest officer of the set walking off to the orchestra to order the dance, while Miss Osborne, passing before her to her little expecting partner, hastily said: "Charles, I beg your pardon for not keeping my engagement, but I am going to dance these two dances with Colonel Beresford. I know you will excuse me and I will certainly dance with you after tea." Without staying for an answer, she turned again to Miss Tomlinson and in another minute was led by Colonel Beresford to begin the set.

If the poor little boy's face had in its happiness been interesting to Emma, it was infinitely more so under this sudden reverse. He stood the picture of disappointment, with crimsoned cheeks, quivering lips and eyes bent on the floor. His mother, stifling her own mortification, tried to soothe his with the prospect of Miss Osborne's second promise but though he contrived to utter, with an effort of boyish bravery, "Oh, I do not mind it!" it was very evident, by the unceasing agitation of his features, that he minded it as much as ever.

Emma did not think or reflect. She felt and acted. "I shall be very happy to dance with you, sir, if you like it," said she, holding out her hand with the most unaffected good humour. The boy, in one moment restored to all his first delight, looked joyfully at his mother and stepping forward with an honest and simple "Thank you, ma'am," was instantly ready to attend his new acquaintance. The thankfulness of Mrs Blake was more diffuse. With a look most expressive of unexpected pleasure and lively gratitude, she turned to her neighbour with repeated and fervent acknowledgements of so great and condescending a kindness to her boy. Emma, with perfect truth, could assure her that she could not be giving greater pleasure than she felt herself. On Charles being provided with his gloves and charged to keep them on, they joined the set which was now rapidly forming, with nearly equal complacency. It was a partnership which could not be noticed without surprise. It gained her a broad stare from Miss Osborne and Miss Tomlinson as they passed her in the dance. "Upon my word, Charles, you are in luck," said the former, as she turned him. "You have got a better partner than me," to which the happy Charles answered, "Yes."

Tom Musgrave, who was dancing with Miss Tomlinson, gave Emma many inquisitive glances and after a time Lord Osborne himself came and, under pretence of talking to Charles, stood to look at his partner. Though rather distressed by such observation, Emma could not repent what she had done, so happy had it made both the boy and his mother, the latter of whom was continually making opportunities of addressing her with the warmest civility. Her little partner, she found, though bent chiefly on dancing, was not unwilling to speak, when her questions or remarks gave him anything to say. She learned, by a sort of inevitable inquiry, that he had two brothers and a sister, that they and their mamma all lived with his uncle, Mr Howard, at Wickstead, that his uncle taught him Latin, that he was very fond of riding and had a horse of his own, a black one, and his uncle had a grey one, given them by Lord Osborne and that he had been out once already with Lord Osborne's hounds.

At the end of these dances, Emma found they were to drink tea. Miss Edwards gave her a caution to be at hand, in a manner which convinced her of Mrs Edwards holding it very important to have them both close to her when she moved into the tea-room. Emma was accordingly on the alert to gain her proper station. It was always the pleasure of the company to have a little bustle and crowd when they adjourned for refreshment. The tea-room was a small room within the card-room and in passing through the latter, where the passage was straitened by tables, Mrs Edwards and her party were for a few moments hemmed in. It happened close by Lady Osborne's cassino table.

Mr Howard, who belonged to it, spoke to his nephew and Emma, on perceiving herself the object of attention both of Lady Osborne and him, had just turned away her eyes in time to avoid seeming to hear her young companion delightedly whisper aloud, "Oh, uncle! do look at my partner; she is so pretty!" As they were immediately in motion again, however, Charles was hurried off without being able to receive his uncle's suffrage. On entering the tea-room, in which two long tables were prepared, Lord Osborne was to be seen quite alone at the end of one, as if retreating as far as he could from the ball, to enjoy his own thoughts and gape without restraint. Charles instantly pointed him out to Emma. "There's Lord Osborne. Let you and I go and sit by him."

"No, no," said Emma, laughing, "you must sit with my friends."

Charles was now free enough to hazard a few questions in his turn. "What o'clock is it?"

"Eleven."

"Eleven! and I am not at all sleepy. Mamma said I should be asleep before ten. How my brothers and sister will envy me! Do you think Miss Osborne will keep her word with me, when tea is over?"

"Oh, yes! I suppose so," though she felt that she had no better reason to give than that Miss Osborne had not kept it before.

"When shall you come to Osborne Castle?"

"Never, probably. I am not acquainted with the family."

"But you may come to Wickstead and see Mamma and she can take you to the castle. There is a monstrous curious stuffed fox there and a badger. Anybody would think they were alive. It is a pity you should not see them."

On rising from tea, there was again a scramble for the pleasure of being first out of the room, which happened to be increased by one or two of the card-parties having just broken up and the players being disposed to move exactly the different way. Among these was Mr Howard, his sister leaning on his arm. No sooner were they within reach of Emma, than Mrs Blake, calling her notice by a friendly touch, said, "Your goodness to Charles, my dear Miss Watson, brings all his family upon you. Give me leave to introduce my brother, Mr Howard." Emma curtsied; the gentleman bowed and made a hasty request for the honour of her hand in the two next dances, to which as hasty an affirmative was given and they were immediately impelled in opposite directions. Emma was very well pleased with the circumstance. There was a quietly cheerful, gentlemanlike air in Mr Howard which suited her and in a few minutes afterwards the value of her engagement increased. As she was sitting in the card-room, somewhat screened by a door, she heard Lord Osborne, who was lounging on a vacant table near her, call Tom Musgrave towards him and say, "I say, Musgrave, why do not you dance with that beautiful Emma Watson? I want you to dance with her and I will come and stand by you."

"I was determining on it this very moment, my lord. I'll be introduced and dance with her directly."

"Aye, do; and if you find she does not want much talking to, you may introduce me by and by."

"Very well, my lord; if she is like her sisters, she will only want to be listened to. I will go this moment. I shall find her in the tea-room. That stiff old Mrs Edwards has never done with tea."

Away he went with Lord Osborne after him and Emma lost no time in hurrying from her corner exactly the other way, forgetting in her haste that she left Mrs Edwards behind.

"We had quite lost you," said Mrs Edwards, who followed her with Mary in less than five minutes. "If you prefer this room to the other, there is no reason why you should not be here but we had better all be together."

Emma was saved the trouble of apologising, by their being joined at the moment by Tom Musgrave. Requesting Mrs Edwards aloud to do him the honour of presenting him to Miss Emma Watson, he left that good lady without any choice in the business, but that of testifying by the coldness of her manner that she did it unwillingly. The honour of dancing with her was solicited without loss of time and Emma, however she might like to be thought a beautiful girl by lord or commoner, was so little disposed to favour Tom Musgrave himself that she had considerable satisfaction in avowing her previous engagement. The style of her last partner had probably led him to believe her not overpowered with applications.

"My little friend Charles Blake," he cried, "must not expect to engross you the whole evening. We can never suffer this. It is against the rules of the assembly and I am sure it will never be patronised by our good friend here, Mrs Edwards. She is by much too nice a judge of decorum to give her license to such a dangerous particularity." To

Emma's amusement Mrs Edwards said nothing but gave him such a look as said that she would prefer Emma to dance with every ten-year-old boy in the county than one dance with him.

"It is not Master Blake that I dance with, sir!"

The gentleman, a little disconcerted, could only hope he might be fortunate another time and seeming unwilling to leave her, though his friend Lord Osborne was waiting in the doorway for the result, as Emma with some amusement perceived, he began to make civil inquiries after her family.

"How comes it that we have not the pleasure of seeing your sisters here this evening? Our assemblies have been used to be so well treated by them that we do not know how to take this neglect."

"My eldest sister is the only one at home and she could not leave my father."

"Miss Elizabeth Watson the only one at home! You astonish me! It seems but the day before yesterday that I saw them all three in this town. But I am afraid I have been a very sad neighbour of late. I hear dreadful complaints of my negligence wherever I go and I confess it is a shameful length of time since I was at Stanton. But I shall now endeavour to make myself amends for the past."

Emma hoped her calm courtesy in reply would strike him as very unlike the encouraging warmth he had received from her sisters and possibly give him the novel sensation of doubting his own influence. The dancing now recommenced. Miss Tomlinson being impatient to call, everybody was required to stand up and Tom Musgrave's curiosity was appeased on seeing Mr Howard come forward and claim Emma's hand.

"That will do as well for me," was Lord Osborne's remark, when his friend carried him the news and he was continually at Howard's elbow during the two dances.

The frequency of his appearance there was the only unpleasant part of the engagement, the only objection she could make to Mr Howard. In himself, she thought him as agreeable as he looked. He had a relaxed, unaffected way of expressing himself and she only regretted that he had not been able to make his former pupil's manners as commendable as his own. His figure and features were as good as the other two men's but it was his almost constant pleasantness that set him apart. It was superior, in fact, by being more ready than Lord Osborne's and more natural than Tom Musgrave's. Their conversation flowed easily and moved from weather to walking, to differences in the Surrey and Shropshire landscapes, to the clear night skies of late. The two dances seemed very short and she had her partner's authority for considering them so.

Mr Howard had gone to fetch Emma a glass of punch when, unseen by the other young men nearby, she overheard their conversation,

"We are off at last," said his lordship to Tom. "How much longer do you stay in this heavenly place – till sunrise?"

"No, faith! my lord. I have had quite enough of it. I assure you, I shall not show myself here again when I have had the honour of attending Lady Osborne to her carriage. I shall retreat in as much secrecy as possible to the most remote corner of the house, where I shall order a barrel of oysters and be famously snug."

"Let me see you soon at the castle and bring me word how she looks by daylight."

Mr Howard returned to Emma and, handing her the glass, expressed regret that he must make an early departure, as he had just learned that the Osbornes were leaving and he must go with them. His kind apology could only impress Emma to greater esteem for him. She had no time to respond, however, as she found herself, in the bustle of the Osbornes' leaving, quite the central character. She and Mrs Blake parted as old acquaintances; Charles shook her by the hand and wished her "goodbye" at least a dozen times. From Miss Osborne she received a brief curtsey as she passed her. Even Lady Osborne gave her a look of complacency and his lordship actually came back, after the others were out of the room, to "beg her pardon" and look in the window seat behind her for the gloves which were visibly compressed in his hand.

As Tom Musgrave was seen no more, Emma supposed his plan to have succeeded and imagined him mortifying with his barrel of oysters in dreary solitude, or gladly assisting the landlady in her bar to make fresh negus for the happy dancers above. Emma could not help missing the party by whom she had been, though in some respects unpleasantly, distinguished and the two dances which followed and concluded the ball were rather flat in comparison with the others. Mr Edwards having played with good luck, they were some of the last in the room.

Just as they arose to depart, they were approached by Solomon Tomlinson who had observed the attention

Emma Watson drew from the Osbornes and was loath to miss out on meeting this stranger of possible consequence. He now requested that Mrs Edwards do him the honour of an introduction. Emma's curtsey was met with the lowest of bows, an uninterested "Watson of Stanton", a hasty "Goodnight" and suddenly he was gone – disappeared behind a large curtain.

CHAPTER FOUR

"Here we are back again, I declare," said Emma sorrowfully, as she walked into the Edwardses' dining-room, where the table was prepared and the neat upper maid was lighting the candles. "My dear Miss Edwards, how soon it is at an end! I wish it could all come over again."

A great deal of kind pleasure was expressed in her having enjoyed the evening so much. Mr Edwards was as warm as herself in the praise of the fullness, brilliancy and spirit of the meeting. Though as he had been fixed the whole time at the same table in the same room, with only one change of chairs, it might have seemed a matter scarcely perceived, but he had won four rubbers out of five and everything went well. His daughter felt the advantage of this gratified state of mind, in the course of the remarks and retrospections which now ensued over the welcome soup.

"How came you not to dance with Mr Tomlinson, Mary?" said her mother.

"I was always engaged when he asked me."

"I thought you were to have stood up with Mr Solomon the two last dances. Mrs Tomlinson told me he was gone to ask you and I had heard you say two minutes before that you were not engaged."

"Yes, but there was a mistake. I had misunderstood. I did not know I was engaged. I thought it had been for the two dances after, if we stayed so long but Captain Hunter assured me it was for those very two."

"So you ended with Captain Hunter, Mary, did you?" said her father. "And whom did you begin with?"

"Captain Hunter," was repeated in a very humble tone.

"Hum! That is being constant, however. But who else did you dance with?"

"Mr Norton and Mr Styles."

"And who are they?"

"Mr Norton is a cousin of Captain Hunter's."

"And who is Mr Styles?"

"One of Captain Hunter's particular friends."

"All in the same regiment," added Mrs Edwards. "Mary was surrounded by red-coats all the evening. I confess, I should have been better pleased to see her dancing with some of our old neighbours."

"Yes, yes. We must not neglect our old neighbours, even if it be Solomon Tomlinson. But if these soldiers are quicker than other people in a ball-room, what are young ladies to do?"

"I think there is no occasion for their engaging themselves so many dances beforehand, Mr Edwards."

"No, perhaps not, but I remember, my dear, when you and I did the same."

"Yes, my dear, and it led to a speedy engagement ... which is not the outcome we are seeking here."

Mrs Edwards said no more and Mary breathed again. A good deal of good-humoured pleasantry followed and Emma went to bed in charming spirits, her head full of Osbornes, Blakes and Howards.

The next morning brought a great many visitors. It was the way of the place always to call on Mrs Edwards the morning after a ball and this neighbourly inclination was increased in the present instance by a general spirit of curiosity on Emma's account. Everybody wanted to look again at the girl who had been admired the night before by Lord Osborne. Many were the eyes and various the degrees of approbation with which she was examined. Some saw no fault and some no beauty. With some her sallow skin was the annihilation of every grace and others could never be persuaded that she was half so handsome as Elizabeth Watson had been ten years ago. The morning passed away quickly in discussing the merits of the ball with all this succession of company and Emma was at once astonished by finding it two o'clock and considering that she had heard nothing of her father's chair. After this discovery, she had walked twice to the window to examine the street and was on the point of asking leave to ring the bell and make inquiries, when the light sound of a carriage driving up to the door set her heart at ease. She stepped again to the window but instead of the unsmart Lady Macbeth-led carriage she perceived a neat curricle. Mr Musgrave was shortly afterwards announced and Mrs Edwards put on her very stiffest look at the sound. Seeming not at all dismayed, however, by her chilling air, he paid his compliments to each of the ladies with no unbecoming ease. Continuing to address Emma, he presented her a note, which he had the honour of bringing from her sister but to which, he must observe, a verbal postscript would be requisite.

The note, which Emma was beginning to read, rather before Mrs Edwards had entreated her to use no ceremony, contained a few lines from Elizabeth importing that their father, in consequence of being unusually well, had taken the sudden resolution of attending the visitation that day. As his road lay quite wide from Dorking, it was impossible for her to come home till the following morning, unless the Edwardses would send her, which was hardly to be expected, or she could meet with any chance conveyance, or did not mind walking so far. She had scarcely run her eye through the whole, before she found herself obliged to listen to Tom Musgrave's further account.

"I received that note from the fair hands of Miss Watson only twenty minutes ago," said he. "I met her in the village of Stanton, whither my good stars prompted me to turn my horses' heads. She was at that moment in quest of a person to employ on the errand and I was fortunate enough to convince her that she could not find a more willing or speedy messenger than myself. Remember, I say nothing of my disinterestedness. My reward is to be the indulgence of conveying you to Stanton in my curricle. Though they are not written down, I bring your sister's orders for the same."

Emma felt distressed. She did not like the proposal for she did not wish to be on terms of intimacy with the proposer. Fearful of encroaching on the Edwardses, however, as well as wishing to go home herself, she was at a loss how entirely to decline what he offered. Mrs Edwards continued silent, either not understanding the case, or waiting to see how the young lady's inclination lay. Emma thanked him but professed herself very unwilling to give him so much trouble. The trouble was of course honour, pleasure, delight. What had he or his horses to do? Still she hesitated. She believed she must beg leave to decline his assistance. She was rather afraid of the sort of carriage. The distance was not beyond a walk. Mrs Edwards was silent no longer. She inquired into the particulars and then said, "We shall be extremely happy, Miss Emma, if you can give us the pleasure of your company till tomorrow but, if you cannot conveniently do so, our carriage is quite at your service and Mary will be pleased with the opportunity of seeing your sister."

This was precisely what Emma had longed for and she accepted the offer most thankfully, acknowledging that as Elizabeth was entirely alone, it was her wish to return home to dinner. The plan was warmly opposed by their visitor.

"I cannot suffer it, indeed. I must not be deprived of the happiness of escorting you. I assure you there is not a possibility of fear with my horses. You might guide them yourself. Your sisters all know how quiet they are. They have none of them the smallest scruple in trusting themselves with me, even on a race-course. Believe me," added he, lowering his voice, "you are quite safe; the danger is only mine."

Emma was not more disposed to oblige him for all this.

"And as to Mrs Edwards' carriage being used the day after a ball, it is a thing quite out of rule, I assure you – never heard of before. The old coachman will look as black as his horses – won't he Miss Edwards?"

No notice was taken. The ladies were silently firm and the gentleman found himself obliged to submit.

"What a famous ball we had last night!" he cried, after a short pause. "How long did you keep it up after the Osbornes and I went away?"

"We had two dances more."

"It is making it too much of a fatigue, I think, to stay so late. I suppose your set was not a very full one."

"Yes. Quite as full as ever, except for the Osbornes. There seemed no vacancy anywhere and everybody danced with uncommon spirit to the very last."

Emma said this, though against her conscience.

"Indeed! Perhaps I might have looked in upon you again, if I had been aware of as much, for I am rather fond of dancing than not. Miss Osborne is a charming girl, is she not?"

"I did not have the opportunity of observing her charm," replied Emma, to whom all this was chiefly addressed.

"Well, let me assure you that she is and her manners are delightful. Although some might say she is not critically handsome, there is that beauty in her which only birth and rank can bestow. And Miss Tomlinson is a most interesting little creature. You can imagine no one more lively. And what do you think of Lord Osborne, Miss Emma?"

"He would be handsome even if he were not a lord."

"Indeed?"

"And perhaps better bred, more desirous of pleasing and showing himself pleased in a right place. He did not dance."

"Upon my word, you are severe upon my friend! I assure you Lord Osborne is a very good fellow."

"I do not dispute his virtues, but merely point to where improvements could be made."

"If it were not a breach of confidence," replied Tom, with an important look, "perhaps I might be able to win a more favourable opinion of poor Osborne."

Emma gave him no encouragement and he was obliged to keep his friend's secret. He was also obliged to put an end to his visit for, Mrs Edwards having ordered her carriage, there was no time to be lost on Emma's side in preparing for it. Miss Edwards accompanied her home but as it was dinner-hour at Stanton, she stayed with them only a few minutes.

"Now, my dear Emma," said Elizabeth, as soon as they were alone, "you must talk to me all the rest of the day without stopping or I shall not be satisfied but, first of all, Nanny shall bring in the dinner. Poor thing! You will not dine as you did yesterday, for we have nothing but some fried beef. How nice Mary Edwards looks in her new pelisse! And now tell me how you like them all and what I am to say to Sam. I have begun my letter. Jack Stokes is to call for it tomorrow for his uncle is going within a mile of Guildford the next day."

Nanny brought in the dinner.

"We will wait upon ourselves," said Elizabeth, "and then we shall lose no time. And so, you would not come home with Tom Musgrave?"

"No, you had said so much against him that I could not wish either for the obligation or the intimacy which the use of his carriage must have created. I should not even have liked the appearance of it. His feelings were not injured, though perhaps his vanity was."

"You did very right, though I wonder at your forbearance and I do not think I could have done it myself. He seemed so eager to fetch you that I could not say no, though it rather went against me to be throwing you together, so well as I knew his tricks. But I did long to see you and it was a clever way of getting you home. Nobody could have thought of the Edwardses letting you have their coach, after the horses being out so late. But what am I to say to Sam?"

"If you are guided by me, you will not encourage him to think of Miss Edwards. The father is decidedly against him, the mother shows him no favour and I doubt his having any interest with Mary. She danced twice with Captain Hunter and I think shows him in general as much encouragement as is consistent with her disposition and the circumstances she is placed in. She once mentioned Sam and certainly with a little confusion but that was perhaps merely owing to the consciousness of his liking her, which may very probably have come to her knowledge."

"Oh, dear! Yes. She has heard enough of that from us all. Poor Sam! He is out of luck as well as other people. For the life of me, Emma, I feel for the broken-hearted. Would that there were some way of knowing that at least one of us is secure. Excepting Robert, we are a hopeless lot. Well, now begin and give me an account of everything as it happened."

Emma obeyed her and Elizabeth listened with very little interruption till she heard of Mr Howard as a partner.

"Dance with Mr Howard! Good Heavens! You don't say so! Why, he is quite one of the great and grand ones. Did you not find him very high?"

"His manners are of a kind to give me much more ease and confidence than Tom Musgrave's."

"Well, go on. I should have been frightened out of my wits to have had anything to do with the Osbornes' set."

Emma concluded her narration.

"And so you really did not dance with Tom Musgrave at all but, really, you must have liked him. He sees himself as irresistible and must never have known such rejection."

"Well he must know it now. I do *not* like him, Elizabeth. I allow his person and air to be good and that his manners to a certain point – his address rather – is pleasing, but I see nothing else to admire in him. On the contrary, he seems very vain, very conceited, absurdly anxious for distinction and absolutely contemptible in some of the measures he takes for becoming so. There is a ridiculousness about him that entertains me but his company gives me no other agreeable emotion."

"My dearest Emma! You are like nobody else in the world. It is well Margaret is not by or what a scene there would be. You do not offend me, though I hardly know how to believe you, but Margaret would never forgive such words."

"I wish Margaret could have heard him profess his ignorance of her being out of the county. He declared it seemed only two days since he had seen her."

"Aye, that is just like him and yet this is the man she will fancy so desperately in love with her. He is no favourite of mine, as you well know. But even I confess, Emma, that he makes me laugh and though I am in no danger of falling for his charms, I acknowledge he is agreeable. Can you lay your hand on your heart and say you do not find him likewise?"

"Indeed, I can, both hands and spread to their widest extent."

"I should like to know the man you do think agreeable."

"His name is Howard."

"Howard! Dear me. I cannot think of him but as playing cards with Lady Osborne and looking proud. I must own, however, that it is a relief to me to find you can speak as you do of Tom Musgrave. My heart did misgive me that you would like him too well. You talked so stoutly beforehand that I was sadly afraid your brag would be punished. I only hope it will last and that he will not come on to pay you much attention. It is a hard thing for a woman to stand against the flattering ways of a man, when he is bent upon pleasing her. Now, what did you think of Miss Osborne and Miss Tomlinson?"

"I could hardly tell. They spoke to none other than each other and the officers who tended them."

"Miss Osborne has personality, cunning and brains enough but Miss Tomlinson has none. She will rattle away when in the company of her friend but is incapable of producing an original thought when away from Miss Osborne, excepting when horses are spoken of as she is an excellent horsewoman. She is not clever, but then she does have the stupidest brother in England."

"Oh Elizabeth, you do speak freely. I hope your wit will never turn on me."

"Of course not. That would never happen, but where I meet with a fool or a blackguard, I cannot help myself. Solomon Tomlinson, in being stupid and having a very high opinion of himself, is one of my most dependable targets."

As their quietly sociable little meal concluded, Elizabeth could not help observing how comfortably it had passed.

"It is so delightful to me," said she, "to have things going on in peace and good humour. Nobody can tell how much I hate quarrelling. Now, though we have had nothing but fried beef, how good it has all seemed! I wish everybody were as easily satisfied as you. Poor Margaret is very snappish and Penelope owns she had rather have quarrelling going on than nothing at all, and when they are cross together – Heavens! I hardly know myself now to be in such pleasant and undemanding company."

This compliment delighted Emma, who reflected how fortunate she was that Elizabeth was the first sister she was reacquainted with and not either of the other two.

Mr Watson returned in the evening not the worse for the exertion of the day and consequently pleased with what he had done and glad to talk of it over his own fireside. Emma had not foreseen any interest to herself in the occurrences of a visitation but when she heard Mr Howard spoken of as the preacher and as having given them an excellent sermon, she could not help listening with a quicker ear.

"I do not know when I have heard a discourse more to my mind," continued Mr Watson, "or one better delivered. He reads extremely well, with great propriety and in a very impressive manner and at the same time without any theatrical grimace or violence. I own I do not like much action in the pulpit. I do not like the studied air and artificial inflexions of voice which your very popular and most admired preachers generally have. I do not trust it. No, I do not trust the arched eyebrow and finger-pointing clergyman. A simple delivery is much better calculated to inspire devotion and shows a much better taste. Mr Howard read like a scholar and a gentleman. They say he may be getting Branchfield in addition to Wickstead. I had been offered Branchfield, Emma, ten years ago but was forced to decline due to poor health. I often think how much better off you girls would be now, had I Branchfield. Stanton is nothing to it."

"And what had you for dinner, sir?" asked his eldest daughter, wishing to change the subject and thus prevent her father's melancholy setting in.

He related the dishes and told what he had eaten himself.

"Upon the whole," he added, "I have had a very comfortable day. My old friends were quite surprised to see me among them and I must say that everybody paid me great attention and seemed to feel for me as an invalid. They would make me sit near the fire and as the partridges were pretty high, Dr Richards would have them sent away to the other end of the table, 'that they might not offend Mr Watson,' which I thought very kind of him. But what pleased me as much as anything was Mr Howard's attention. There is a pretty steep flight of steps up to the room we dine in, which do not quite agree with my gouty foot, and Mr Howard walked by me from the bottom to the top and would make me take his arm. It struck me as very becoming in so young a man but I am sure I had no claim to expect it, for I never saw him before in my life. By the by, he inquired after one of my daughters but I do not know which. I suppose you know among yourselves."

CHAPTER FIVE

On the third day after the ball, as Nanny, at five minutes before three, was beginning to bustle into the parlour with the tray and knife-case, she was suddenly called to the front door by the sound of as smart a rap as the end of a riding-whip could give. Though charged by Elizabeth to let nobody in, she returned in half a minute with a look of awkward dismay to hold the parlour door open for Lord Osborne and Tom Musgrave. The surprise of the young ladies may be imagined. No visitors would have been welcome at such a moment but such visitors as these – such a one as Lord Osborne at least, a nobleman and a stranger – was really distressing.

He looked a little embarrassed himself as, on being introduced by his easy, voluble friend, he muttered something of doing himself the honour of waiting upon Mr Watson. Though Emma could not but take the compliment of the visit to herself, she was very far from enjoying it. She felt all the inconsistency of such an acquaintance with the very humble style in which they were obliged to live. Having in her aunt's family been used to many of the elegancies of life, she was fully sensible of all that must be open to the ridicule of richer people in her present home. Of the pain of such feelings, Elizabeth knew very little. Her simple viewpoint, or juster reason, saved her from such mortification; and though shrinking under a general sense of inferiority, she felt no particular shame.

Mr Watson, as the gentlemen had already heard from Nanny, was not well enough to be downstairs. With much concern they took their seats, Lord Osborne near Emma and the convenient Mr Musgrave, in high spirits, on the other side of the fireplace, with Elizabeth. When Lord Osborne had hoped that Emma had not caught cold at the ball, he had nothing more to say for some time and could only gratify his eye by occasional glances at his fair neighbour. Emma was not inclined to give herself much trouble for his entertainment and after hard labour of mind, he produced the remark of it being a very fine day and followed it up with the question of, "Have you been walking this morning?"

"No, my lord, we thought it too dirty."

"You should wear half-boots." After another pause, "Nothing sets off a neat ankle more than a half-boot; nankeen galoshed with black looks very well. Do not you like half-boots?"

"Yes, but unless they are so stout as to injure their beauty, they are not fit for country walking."

"Ladies should ride in dirty weather. Do you ride?"

"No, my lord."

"I wonder every lady does not. A woman never looks better than on horseback."

"But every woman may not have the inclination, or the means."

"If they knew how much it became them, they would all have the inclination and I fancy, Miss Watson, when once they had the inclination, the means would soon follow."

"Your lordship thinks we always have our own way. That is a point on which ladies and gentlemen have long disagreed. Without pretending to decide it, I may say that there are some circumstances which even *women* cannot control. Female economy will do a great deal, my lord, but it cannot turn a small income into a large one."

Lord Osborne was silenced. Her manner had been neither critical nor sarcastic but there was a something in its mild seriousness, as well as in the words themselves, which made his lordship think. When he addressed her again, it was with a degree of considerate propriety totally unlike the half-awkward, half-fearless style of his former remarks. It was a new thing with him to wish to please a woman. It was the first time that he had ever felt what was due to a woman in Emma's situation but as he wanted neither in sense nor a good disposition, he did not feel it without effect.

"You have not been long in this country, I understand," said he, in the tone of a gentleman. "I hope you are pleased with it."

He was rewarded by a gracious answer and a more liberal full view of her face than she had yet bestowed. Unused to exert himself and happy in contemplating her, he then sat in silence for some minutes longer. Tom Musgrave continued chattering to Elizabeth till they were interrupted by the approach of Nanny, who, half-opening the door and putting in her head, said, "Please, ma'am, master wants to know why he ben't to have his dinner?"

The gentlemen, who had hitherto disregarded every symptom, however positive, of the nearness of that meal, now jumped up with apologies, while Elizabeth, much to Emma's embarrassment, called briskly after Nanny to "tell Betty to take up the fowls."

"I am sorry it happens so," Elizabeth continued, turning good-humouredly towards Musgrave, "but you know what early hours we keep."

Tom had nothing to say for himself. He knew it very well and such honest simplicity, such shameless truth, rather bewildered him. Lord Osborne's parting compliments took some time – his inclination for speech seeming to increase with the shortness of the term for indulgence. He recommended exercise in defiance of dirt, spoke again in praise of half-boots and begged that his sister might be allowed to send Emma the name of her shoemaker. He concluded with saying, "My hounds will be hunting this country in early December. I believe they will throw off at Stanton Wood on the first Tuesday at nine o'clock. I mention this in hopes of your being drawn out to see what's going on. If the morning is tolerable, pray do us the honour of giving us your good wishes in person."

The sisters looked on each other with astonishment when their visitors had withdrawn.

"Here's an unaccountable honour!" cried Elizabeth, at last. "Who would have thought of Lord Osborne's coming to Stanton? He is very handsome but Tom Musgrave looks all to nothing the smartest and most fashionable man of the two. I am glad he did not say anything to me. I would not have had to talk to such a great man for the world. I might have said anything. Tom was very agreeable, was he not? But did you hear him ask where Miss Penelope and Miss Margaret were, when he first came in? It put me out of patience. I am glad Nanny had not laid the cloth, however; it would have looked so awkward. Just the tray did not signify."

To say that Emma was not flattered by Lord Osborne's visit would be to assert a very unlikely thing and describe a very odd young lady. His coming was a sort of notice which might please her vanity but did not suit her pride and she would rather have known that he wished the visit without presuming to make it, than have seen him at Stanton.

Among other unsatisfactory feelings, it once occurred to her to wonder why Mr Howard had not taken the same privilege of coming and accompanied his lordship. She was willing to suppose that he had either known nothing about it or had declined any share in a measure which carried quite as much impertinence in its form as good-breeding. Mr Watson was very far from being delighted when he heard what had passed. A little peevish under immediate pain and ill-disposed to be pleased, he only replied,

"Phoo! phoo! What occasion could there be for Lord Osborne's coming? I have lived here many years without being noticed by any of the family. It is some foolery of that idle fellow, Tom Musgrave. I cannot return the visit. I would not if I could. What do they mean making an old man feel his decline so?"

When Tom Musgrave was met with again, he was commissioned with a message of excuse to Osborne Castle on the too-sufficient plea of Mr Watson's infirm state of health.

CHAPTER SIX

A week or ten days rolled quietly away after this visit before any new bustle arose to interrupt even for half a day the tranquil and affectionate intercourse of the two sisters. Their mutual regard was increasing with the intimate knowledge of each other which such intercourse produced. Emma delighted in Elizabeth's warmth and wit while Elizabeth soon discovered a pleasant companion, happy to share the burden of caring for an invalid parent but who also had a particular talent for teasing their father into good humour. The first circumstance to indicate a change was the receipt of a letter from Croydon to announce the speedy return of Margaret and a visit of two or three days from Mr and Mrs Robert Watson, who undertook to bring her home and wished to see their sister Emma.

It was an expectation to fill the thoughts of the sisters at Stanton and to busy the hours of one of them at least. As Jane had been a woman of fortune, the preparations for her entertainment were considerable and as Elizabeth had at all times more goodwill than method in her guidance of the house, she saw no domestic alterations necessary.

An absence of fourteen years had made all her brothers

and sisters strangers to Emma, but in her expectation of Margaret there was more than the awkwardness of such an alienation. She had heard things which made her dread her return and the day which brought the party to Stanton seemed to her the probable conclusion of almost all that had been comfortable in the house. She failed to see how the intimacy of a pair of loving sisters could admit a third, whose character was bent on disquiet and trouble.

Robert Watson was an attorney at Croydon, in a good way of business. He was very well satisfied with himself for the same and for having married the only daughter of the attorney to whom he had been clerk, with a fortune of six thousand pounds. Mrs Robert was not less pleased with herself for having had that six thousand pounds and for being now in possession of a very smart house in Croydon, where she gave genteel parties and wore fine clothes. In her person there was nothing remarkable – her manners were pert and conceited.

Margaret was not without beauty. She had a slight pretty figure, tight dark curls and rather wanted countenance than good features but the sharp and anxious expression of her face made her beauty, in general, little felt. On meeting her long-absent sister, as on every occasion of show, her manner was all affection and her voice all insincere with exaggerated gentleness, continuous smiles and a very slow articulation being her constant resource when determined on pleasing.

She was now so "delighted to see dear, dear Emma," that she could hardly speak a word in a minute.

"I am sure we shall be very great friends," Margaret

observed with much sentiment, as they were sitting together. Emma scarcely knew how to answer such a proposition and could not meet it with equal enthusiasm.

Mrs Robert Watson eyed Emma with much familiar curiosity and triumphant compassion. The loss of the aunt's fortune was uppermost in her mind at the moment of meeting and she could not but feel how much better it was to be the daughter of a gentleman of property in Croydon than the niece of an old woman who threw herself away on an Irish captain.

Robert was carelessly kind, as became a prosperous man and a brother. He was more intent on settling with the post-boy, inveighing against the exorbitant advance in posting and pondering over a doubtful half-crown declaring he would whip the boy if it were a fake, than on welcoming a sister who was no longer likely to have any property for him to get the direction of.

"Your road through the village is infamous, Elizabeth," said he. "Worse than ever it was. By Heaven! I would indict it if I lived near you. Who is surveyor now?"

There was a little niece at Croydon to be fondly inquired after by the kind-hearted Elizabeth, who regretted very much her not being of the party.

"You are very good," replied her mother, "and I assure you it went very hard with Augusta to have us come away without her. I was forced to say we were only going to church and promise to come back for her directly. But you know it would not do to bring her without her maid and I am as particular as ever in having her properly attended to."

"Sweet little darling!" cried Margaret. "It quite broke my heart to leave her."

"Then why were you in such a hurry to run away from her?" cried Mrs Robert. "You are a sad, shabby girl. I have been quarrelling with you all the way we came, have I not? Such a visit as this, I never heard of! You know how glad we are to have any of you with us, if it be for months together. I am sorry" (with a witty smile) "we have not been able to make Croydon agreeable this autumn."

"My dearest Jane, do not overpower me with your raillery. You know what inducements I had to bring me home. Spare me, I entreat you. I am no match for your arch sallies."

"Well, I only beg you will not set your neighbours against the place. Perhaps Emma may be tempted to go back with us and stay till Christmas, if you don't put in your word."

Jane Watson, having installed a good nanny, was quite at her leisure to exhibit her husband's sisters as she had none of her own. Feeling all the consequence and importance of superiority in all the areas that mattered, she was quite determined to do so.

Emma was greatly obliged.

"I assure you we have very good society at Croydon. I do not much attend the balls, they are rather too mixed, but our parties are very select and good. I had seven tables last week in my drawing-room. Are you fond of the country? How do you like Stanton?"

"Very much," replied Emma, who thought a comprehensive answer most to the purpose. She saw that her sister-in-law despised her immediately. Mrs Robert

Watson was indeed wondering what sort of a home Emma could possibly have been used to in Shropshire and setting it down as certain that the aunt could never have had six thousand pounds.

"How charming Emma is," whispered Margaret to Mrs Robert, in her most languishing tone. Emma was becoming annoyed by such insincerity and she did not like it better when she heard Margaret five minutes afterwards say to Elizabeth in a sharp, quick accent, totally unlike the first, "Have you heard from Pen since she went to Chichester? I had a letter the other day. I don't find she is likely to make anything of it. I fancy she'll come back 'Miss Penelope', as she went."

Such, she feared, would be Margaret's common voice when the novelty of her own appearance were over. The tone of artificial sensibility was not recommended by the idea. The ladies were invited upstairs to prepare for dinner.

"I hope you will find things tolerably comfortable, Jane," said Elizabeth, as she opened the door of the spare bedchamber.

"My good creature," replied Jane, "use no ceremony with me, I entreat you. I am one of those who always take things as they find them. I hope I can put up with a small apartment for two or three nights without making a piece of work. I always wish to be treated quite en famille when I come to see you. And now I do hope you have not been getting a great dinner for us. Remember, we never eat suppers."

"I suppose," said Margaret, rather quickly to Emma, "you and I are to be together. Elizabeth always takes care to have a room to herself."

"No. Elizabeth gives me half hers."

"Oh!" in a softened voice and rather mortified to find that she was not ill-used. "I am sorry I am not to have the pleasure of your company, especially as it makes me nervous to be much alone."

Emma was the first of the females in the parlour again. On entering it she found her brother alone.

"So, Emma," said he, "you are quite a stranger at home. It must seem odd enough for you to be here. A pretty piece of work your Aunt Turner has made of it! By Heaven! A woman should never be trusted with money. I always said she ought to have settled something on you, as soon as her husband died."

"But that would have been trusting me with money," replied Emma, "and I am a woman too."

"It might have been secured to your future use, or a husband's, without your having any power over it now. What a blow it must have been upon you! To find yourself, instead of heiress of eight or nine thousand pounds, sent back a weight upon your family, without a sixpence. I hope the old woman will smart for it."

"Please do not speak disrespectfully of her; she was very good to me and if she has made an imprudent choice, she will suffer more from it herself than I can possibly do."

"I do not mean to distress you," although in fact he did, for the whole business angered him and he wished to lay some share of the responsibility at her door, "but you know everybody must think her an old fool. I thought Turner had been reckoned an extraordinarily sensible, clever man. How the devil came he to make such a will?"

"My uncle's sense is not at all impeached in my opinion by his attachment to my aunt. She had been an excellent wife to him. The most liberal and enlightened minds are always the most confiding. The event has been unfortunate but my uncle's memory is, if possible, endeared to me by such a proof of tender respect for my aunt."

"That's odd sort of talking. He might have provided decently for his widow, without leaving everything that he had to dispose of, or any part of it, at her mercy."

"You know," replied Emma, struggling with her tears, "my uncle's melancholy state of health. He was a greater invalid than my father. He could not leave home. Please do not speak of him so. My aunt may have erred," said Emma warmly, "she has erred, but my uncle's conduct was faultless. I was her own niece and he left to herself the power and the pleasure of providing for me."

"But unluckily they have now left the pleasure of providing for you to your father. That's the long and short of the business. After keeping you at a distance from your family for such a length of time as must do away all natural affection among us. Breeding you up, I suppose, in a superior style, you are returned upon their hands without a sixpence and little to recommend you. How can you hope to marry well? And if you girls do not marry, who is to provide for you in the future? I certainly have not made provisions for it and I very much doubt that Sam has done so. I have a growing family and why should I suffer and an Irish captain gain? No, you had all best marry and soon."

So contrary a sentiment to what Emma had expected on reuniting, at last, with a brother, and her powerlessness to relieve the circumstances to which he alluded, affected her greatly and she could hold the tears back no longer.

"I do not mean to make you cry," said Robert, rather softened, and after a short silence, by way of changing the subject, he added, "I am just come from my father's room. He seems very indifferent. It will be a sad break up when he dies. Elizabeth will be quite useless when he is gone ... and old. Pity you can none of you get married! You must come to Croydon as well as the rest and see what you can do there. I believe if Margaret had had a thousand or fifteen hundred pounds, there was a young man who would have thought of her. We will do our best to find you a husband, however things may turn out for Elizabeth ... there, now, are we not good to you?"

Emma was glad when they were soon joined by the others. It was better to look at her sister-in-law's finery than listen to Robert, who had irritated and grieved her in equal measure. Mrs Robert, exactly as smart as she had been at her own party, came in with apologies for her dress.

"I would not make you wait," said she, "so I put on the first thing I met with. I am afraid I am a sad figure. My dear Mr W.," (to her husband) "you have not put any fresh powder in your hair."

"No, I do not intend it. I think there is powder enough in my hair for my wife and sisters."

"Indeed, you ought to make some alteration in your dress before dinner when you are out visiting, though you do not at home."

"Nonsense."

"It is very odd you should not like to do what other gentlemen do. Mr Marshall and Mr Hemmings change their dress every day of their lives before dinner. And what was the use of my putting up your last new coat, if you are never to wear it?"

"Do be satisfied with being fine yourself and leave your husband alone."

To put an end to this altercation and soften the evident vexation of her sister-in-law, Emma (though in no spirits to make such nonsense easy) began to admire her gown. It produced immediate complacency.

"Do you like it?" said she. "I am very happy. It has been excessively admired but sometimes I think the pattern too large. I shall wear one tomorrow that I think you will prefer to this. Have you seen the one I gave Margaret?"

Dinner came and except when Mrs Robert looked at her husband's head, she continued gay and flippant, chiding Elizabeth for the profusion on the table and absolutely protesting against the entrance of the roast turkey.

"I do beg and entreat that no turkey may be seen today. I am really frightened out of my wits with the number of dishes we have already. Let us have no turkey, I beseech you."

"My dear Jane," replied Elizabeth, "the turkey is even now roasted and it may just as well come in and join us, as have it snubbed in the kitchen. Besides, if it is cut, I am in hopes my father may be tempted to eat a bit, for it is rather a favourite dish."

"You may have it in, my dear; but I assure you I shan't touch it, but a little," and a short time later, Jane Watson could be seen helping herself to a large portion of the very fowl she was so vehemently against.

Mr Watson had not been well enough to join the party at dinner but was prevailed on to come down and drink tea with them.

"I wish we may be able to have a game of cards tonight," said Elizabeth to Mrs Robert, after seeing her father comfortably seated in his armchair.

"Not on my account, my dear, I beg. You know I am no card-player. I think a snug chat infinitely better. I always say cards are very well sometimes to break a formal circle but one never wants them among friends."

"I was thinking of it as being something to amuse my father," said Elizabeth, "if it was not disagreeable to you. He says his head won't bear whist but perhaps if we make a round game he may be tempted to sit down with us."

"By all means, my dear creature, I am quite at your service, only do not oblige me to choose the game, that's all. Speculation is the only round game at Croydon now but I can play anything. When there is only one or two of you at home, you must be quite at a loss to amuse him. Why do you not get him to play at cribbage? Margaret and I have played at cribbage most nights that we have not been engaged."

A sound like a distant carriage was at this moment caught. Everybody listened – it became more decided. It certainly drew nearer. It was an unusual sound for Stanton at any time of the day, for the village was on no very public road and contained no gentleman's family but the rector's. The wheels rapidly approached. In two minutes the general expectation was answered. They stopped beyond a doubt at the garden-gate of the parsonage. Who could it be? It was certainly a carriage. Penelope was the only creature to be thought of. She might perhaps have met with some unexpected opportunity of returning. A pause of suspense ensued. Steps were distinguished along the paved foot-way, which led under the windows of the house to the front door and then within the passage. They were the steps of a man. It could not be Penelope. It must be Samuel.

The door opened and displayed Tom Musgrave in the wrap of a traveller. He had been in London and was now on his way home and he had come half a mile out of his road merely to call for ten minutes at Stanton. He loved to take people by surprise with sudden visits at extraordinary seasons. In the present instance, he had the additional motive of being able to tell the Miss Watsons, whom he depended on finding sitting quietly employed after tea, that he was going home to an eight o'clock dinner.

As it happened, however, he did not give more surprise than he received. Instead of being shown into the usual little sitting-room, the door of the best parlour (a foot larger each way than the other) was thrown open and he beheld a circle of smart people whom he could not immediately recognise arranged, with all the honours of visiting, round the fire. Elizabeth, he observed, was seated at the best Pembroke table, with the best tea-things before her. He stood a few seconds in silent amazement. "Musgrave!" ejaculated Margaret, in a tender voice. "Musgrave!" muttered her father, in a less than impressed one. Tom recollected himself and came forward, delighted to find such a circle of friends and blessing his good fortune for the unlooked-for indulgence. He shook hands with Robert, bowed and smiled to the ladies and did everything very prettily. As to any particularity of address or emotion towards Margaret, Emma, who closely observed him, perceived nothing that did not justify Elizabeth's opinion, though Margaret's modest smiles imported that she meant to take the visit to herself. He was persuaded without much difficulty to throw off his great-coat and drink tea with them. For whether he dined at eight or nine, as he observed, "was a matter of very little consequence", and without seeming to seek, he did not turn away from the chair close by Margaret, which she was assiduous in providing him. She had thus secured him from her sisters, but it was not immediately in her power to preserve him from her brother's claims. Musgrave had come from London and left it only hours before; the last current report as to public news and the general opinion of the day must be understood before Robert could let his attention be yielded to the less national and important demands of the women. At last, however, he was at liberty to hear Margaret's soft address, as she spoke her fears of his having had a most terrible cold, dark, dreadful journey.

"Indeed, you should not have set out so late!"

"I fear I could not be here earlier," he replied. "I was detained chatting at the Bedford by a friend. All hours are alike to me. How long have you been in the country, Miss Margaret?"

"We only came this morning. My kind brother and sister brought me home this very morning. 'Tis singular, is it not?"

"You were gone a great while, were not you? A fortnight, I suppose?"

"You may call a fortnight a great while, Mr Musgrave," said Mrs Robert, sharply; "but we think a month very little. I assure you we bring her home at the end of a month much against our will."

"A month! Have you really been gone a month? 'Tis amazing how time flies."

"You may imagine," said Margaret, in a sort of whisper, "what are my sensations in finding myself once more at Stanton. You know what a sad visitor I make. And I was so excessively impatient to see Emma. I dreaded the meeting and at the same time longed for it. Do you not comprehend the sort of feeling?"

"Not at all," cried he aloud, "I could never dread a meeting with Miss Emma Watson … or any of her sisters."

It was lucky that he added that finish.

"Were you speaking to me?" said Emma, who had caught her own name.

"Not absolutely," he answered, "but I was thinking of you, as many at a greater distance are probably doing at this moment. Fine open weather, Miss Emma, charming season for hunting."

"Emma is delightful, is she not?" whispered Margaret. "I have found her more than answering my warmest hopes. Did you ever see anything more perfectly beautiful? I think even you must be a convert to a brown complexion."

He hesitated. Margaret was fair herself and he did not particularly want to compliment her but Miss Osborne and Miss Tomlinson were likewise fair and his devotion to them carried the day.

"Your sister's complexion," said he, at last, "is as fine as a dark complexion can be but I still profess my preference of a fair skin. You have seen Miss Osborne? She is my model for a truly feminine complexion and she is very fair."

"Is she fairer than me?"

Tom made no reply. "Upon my honour, ladies," said he, giving a glance over his own person, "I am highly indebted to your condescension for admitting me in such *déshabillé* into your drawing-room. I really did not consider how unfit I was to be here, or I hope I should have kept my distance. Lady Osborne would tell me that I were growing as careless as her son, if she saw me in this condition."

The ladies were not wanting in civil returns and Robert Watson, stealing a view of his own head in an opposite glass, said with equal civility, "You cannot be more in *déshabillé* than myself. We got here so late that I had not time even to put a little fresh powder in my hair."

Emma could not help entering into what she supposed were her sister-in-law's feelings at the moment.

When the tea-things were removed, Tom began to talk of his carriage. The old card-table was set out, however, and the general voice was so urgent with him to join their party that he agreed to allow himself another quarter of an hour. Even Emma was pleased that he would stay for she was beginning to feel that a family party might be the worst of all parties, and the others were delighted.

"What's your game?" cried he, as they stood round the table.

"Speculation, I believe," said Elizabeth. "My sister recommends it and I fancy we all like it. I know you do, Tom."

"It is the only round game played at Croydon now," said Mrs Robert. "We never think of any other. I am glad it is a favourite with you."

"Oh, me!" said Tom. "Whatever you decide on will be a favourite with *me*. I have had some pleasant hours at Speculation in my time but I have not been in the way of it now for a long while. Vingt-un is the game at Osborne Castle. I have played nothing but Vingt-un of late. You would be astonished to hear the noise we make there – the fine old lofty drawing-room rings again. Lady Osborne sometimes declares she cannot hear herself speak. Lord Osborne enjoys it famously and he makes the best dealer without exception that I ever beheld – such quickness and spirit, he lets nobody dream over their cards. I wish you could see him overdraw himself on both his own cards. It is worth anything in the world!"

"Dear me!" cried Margaret. "Why should not we play at Vingt-un? I think it is a much better game than Speculation. I cannot say I am very fond of Speculation."

Mrs Robert offered not another word in support of the game. She was quite vanquished and the fashions of Osborne Castle carried it over the fashions of Croydon.

"Do you see much of the parsonage family at the castle, Mr Musgrave?" said Emma, as they were taking their seats.

"Oh, yes, they are almost always there. Mrs Blake is a nice little, good-humoured woman. She and I are sworn friends and Howard's a very gentlemanlike, good sort of fellow! You are not forgotten, I assure you, by any of the party. I fancy you must have a little cheek-glowing now and then, Miss Emma. Were you not rather warm last Saturday about nine or ten o'clock in the evening? I will tell you how it was, I see you are dying to know. Says Howard to Lord Osborne …"

At this interesting moment he was called on by the others to regulate the game and determine some disputable point. His attention was so totally engaged in the business and afterwards by the course of the game, as never to revert to what he had been saying, and Emma, though suffering a good deal from curiosity, dared not remind him.

He proved a very useful addition to their table and Emma marvelled at how truly gifted this man was. If one could have a purpose in life – to be entertaining and charming in company, to put everyone at ease and good humour – then Tom Musgrave had found his. Without him, it would have been a party of such very near relations as could have felt little interest and perhaps maintained little complaisance. His presence among them, however, gave variety and secured good manners. There was no danger of Margaret and Jane squabbling or Robert lecturing while he was present. Tom Musgrave was, in fact, excellently qualified to shine at a round game and few situations made him appear to greater advantage. He played with spirit and had a great deal to say. Though no wit himself, he could sometimes make use of the wit of an absent friend and had a lively way of retailing a common-place or saying a mere nothing, that had great effect at a card-table. The ways and good jokes of Osborne Castle were now added to his ordinary means of entertainment. He repeated the smart sayings of one lady, detailed the oversights of another and indulged them even with a copy of Lord Osborne's style of overdrawing himself on both cards.

The clock struck nine while he was thus agreeably occupied and when Nanny came in with her master's basin of gruel, he had the pleasure of observing to Mr Watson that he should leave him at supper while he went home to dinner himself. The carriage was ordered to the door and no entreaties for his staying longer could now avail. He well knew that if he stayed he must sit down to supper in less than ten minutes, which to a man whose heart had been long fixed on calling his next meal a dinner, was quite insupportable. On finding him determined to go, Margaret began to wink and nod at Elizabeth to ask him to dinner for the following day. Elizabeth at last, not able to resist hints which her own hospitable, social temper more than half seconded, gave the invitation: Would he give them the meeting, they should be very happy.

"With the greatest pleasure," was his first reply. In a moment afterwards: "That is, if I can possibly get here in time but I shoot with Lord Osborne and therefore must not engage. You will not think of me unless you see me." And so he departed, delighted with the uncertainty in which he had left the matter, leaving the others, excepting Mr Watson who was now preoccupied with his gruel, in a glow of "fine fellow" and "charming".

Margaret, in the joy of her heart under circumstances which she chose to consider as peculiarly propitious, would willingly have made a confidante of Emma when they were alone for a short time the next morning. She had even proceeded so far as to say, "The young man who was here last night, my dear Emma, and returns today, is more interesting to me than perhaps you may be aware ..." But Emma, pretending to understand nothing extraordinary in the words, made some very inapplicable reply and, jumping up, ran away from a subject which was odious to her feelings. As Margaret would not allow a doubt to be repeated of Musgrave's coming to dinner, preparations were made for his entertainment much exceeding what had been deemed necessary the day before and taking the office of superintendence entirely from her sister, she was half the morning in the kitchen herself, directing and scolding.

After a great deal of indifferent cooking and anxious suspense, however, they were obliged to sit down without their guest. Tom Musgrave never came. Nanny, as she moved about noisily clearing the dining table, could be heard muttering about the fickleness of young men and the waste of good joints of beef. Margaret was at no pains to conceal her vexation under the disappointment, or repress the peevishness of her temper. The peace of the party for the remainder of that day and the whole of the next, which comprised the length of Robert and Jane's visit, was continually invaded by her fretful displeasure and querulous attacks. Elizabeth was the usual targeted object of both. Margaret had just respect enough for the opinion of her brother and sister-in-law to behave properly by them but Elizabeth and the maids could never do anything right. Emma, whom she seemed no longer to think about, found the continuance of the gentle voice beyond her calculation, short.

Eager to be as little among them as possible, Emma was delighted with the alternative of sitting above with her father and warmly entreated to be his constant companion each evening. Elizabeth loved company of any kind too well not to prefer being below at all risks. She had rather talk of Croydon with Jane, with every interruption of Margaret's perverseness, than sit with only her father and as soon as she could be persuaded to believe it no sacrifice on her sister's part, she was content with the arrangement.

To Emma, the change was most acceptable and delightful. Her father, if ill, required little more than gentleness and silence and being a man of sense and education, was, if able to converse, a welcome companion. In his chamber Emma was at peace from the dreadful mortifications of ill-breeding and family discord − from the immediate endurance of hard-hearted prosperity, low-minded conceit and wrong-headed folly. She still suffered from them in the contemplation of their existence, in memory and in prospect, but, for the moment, she ceased to be tortured by their effects. In Elizabeth, at least, she had found a companion who, if they could be left alone to enjoy the company of the other, she was confident would more than make up for the shortcomings of the rest of her family. Elizabeth's affection for her was sincere. It was balm for the hurt and humiliation she had felt at having to impose upon them when all had hoped that her future would secure and strengthen theirs.

The change in her home, society and style of life, in consequence of the death of one friend and the imprudence of another, had indeed been striking. She had been the first object of hope to an uncle who had formed her mind with the care of a parent and of tenderness to an aunt whose amiable temper had delighted to give her every indulgence.

She was no longer the life and spirit of a house where all had been comfort, freedom and elegance. The expected heiress of an easy independence, she had become of importance to no one. She was now a burden on those whose affections she could not expect – an addition in a house already overstocked, with little hope of future support. It was well for her that she was naturally cheerful, for the change in her situation, if dwelled on for long, had been such as might have plunged weak spirits into despondence. When contrasting the past and the present, therefore, the employment of mind which only reading could produce made Emma gratefully and frequently turn to a book.

She was very much pressed by Robert and Jane to return with them to Croydon and had some difficulty in getting a refusal accepted, as they thought too highly of their own kindness and situation to suppose the offer could appear in a less advantageous light to anybody else. Elizabeth gave them her interest, though evidently against her own, in privately urging Emma to go.

"You do not know what you refuse, Emma," said she, "nor what you have to bear at home. I would advise you by all means to accept the invitation. There is always something lively going on at Croydon. You will be in company almost every day and Robert and Jane will be very kind to you. As for me, I shall be no worse off without you than I had been before, but Margaret's disagreeable ways are new to you and they would vex you more than you know."

Emma was of course uninfluenced, except to greater esteem for Elizabeth, by such representations and the visitors departed without her.

CHAPTER SEVEN

Mr Watson's living, transferable to another clergyman on his death, afforded him five hundred pounds per year with which to maintain the appearance of a gentleman. With this modest sum and a large family he had, over the years, made valiant but largely unsuccessful attempts to keep his home in good repair. Hopes centred on his younger son, Sam, taking orders and thereby, in securing the living and house, providing protection for his sisters. But being a liberal man and having lost his sensible wife while his children were still young, Mr Watson made no outward objection when Sam declared his intention to study medicine. Emma, after all, would save them. But here she was, returned to Stanton, with less in her purse than when she had left it fourteen years before.

"I hope, my dear Emma," said Elizabeth as they sat down to breakfast one morning, "that you have been perfecting your Vingt-un for I have reason to expect an addition to our company. I received a letter this morning with all the particulars."

"Who can you mean?"

"Why, you must guess, of course."

"Sam. It is Sam, surely."

"No, I am afraid not. Sam works too hard and is determined to do well so we do not see him often. You must guess again."

"Robert visited recently; therefore, it must be Penelope."

"Yes, it is Penelope, and in the company of a gentleman."

"She is wed?"

"Yes, married to a Dr Harding. She is cunning and has had her way at last. They are to stay at the inn at Dorking."

This was good news indeed for, in their residing elsewhere, Emma would be spared the trouble of becoming intimate with the sister she was most frightened of. The domestic quietude that she and Elizabeth enjoyed, even with Margaret, the principal quarreller, at home would almost definitely be upended if Penelope returned to the nest. It was with great enthusiasm, therefore, that she said, "Why, this is marvellous news!"

"Yes, and they are to continue to live in Chichester, for the doctor has a fine house there which I should like to visit someday. Penelope longs to pay a visit to Stanton so that her husband may meet with Father. And, I am convinced, to show off her wealthy husband to all her old friends. So they come next Tuesday and bring the doctor's niece and nephew with them. We will meet often, I dare say. What a wonderful thing!"

Emma could tell by how Elizabeth's eyes lit up that the "wonderful thing" she referred to was not Penelope's return to the homestead. It was, rather, the promise of visitors, some of whom were unknown to them and would thus widen their circle of acquaintance for a time and enliven their otherwise dull days. As if she read Emma's thoughts, Elizabeth added,

"Oh my word, visitors means visiting. Such toing and froing as we have not had in years at Stanton. Why, Miss Shaw may be a delightful girl and her brother may be handsome, rich and ready to fall in love. I shall include them both in my evening prayers that we will find them so. But remember what I mentioned to you about Penelope," said Elizabeth, leaving the room, "do not trust her for an instant."

Meanwhile, it seemed that when Margaret was not sighing and complaining, she was finding excuses not to tend to their father. Emma marvelled at the lengths she would go to, to create obstacles and devise cunning escapes. The period of novelty in reacquainting herself with Emma had not lasted long, as Emma had predicted. Margaret had clearly discovered there was little in the relationship that could further her own interests and so the most natural thing was to commence her criticism and complaints.

"I do not see why I should not get the carriage tomorrow for my trip to town, Elizabeth."

"I have already told you. Emma requested it first as she is to return a visit to Miss Edwards in the morning."

Margaret stamped her foot. "But I am older and therefore have seniority in decisions that affect this household. This was not even her home until recently, for her to make demands of its occupants. How dare she take the carriage from me."

"She does not take it from you. I told her she may have it," Elizabeth answered, not taking her eye from her needlework and in the calm tone of one who had to regularly deal with such outbursts.

"I have heard it from Mrs Price that Tom Musgrave has been seen in town every Thursday of late, for that is when Lord Osborne goes there on business. Perhaps I would have met him there tomorrow. Nobody thinks of me."

"Margaret, you may have the carriage in the afternoon, which is best, for everyone knows that the Osbornes rise late. They arrive in town only when most businesses are closing for the day. You must acknowledge that there is a greater likelihood of old Lady Macbeth winning Ascot than of Tom Musgrave and the Osbornes being in town before noon."

This comment silenced Margaret for she saw the sense in it. It would be dreadful to arrive too early and miss an opportunity for a chance meeting with Tom Musgrave.

"Very well," she conceded. "I will take the carriage in the afternoon but in future Emma is to consult me first."

Miss Edwards was exceedingly pleased to chat with Emma again, in particular about the ball at which they had last met and about the next ball which was fast approaching. Mrs Edwards was called to the library by her husband to look over a letter of importance before he dispatched it, so they were left in the large part to themselves. And where young ladies are left unattended to discuss balls, the conversation naturally tends towards the discussion of young men. Having agreed that Captain Hunter was the most distinguished looking gentleman of the evening and that Mr Howard was not proud in the least but quite the opposite, Miss Edwards brought the conversation to

Emma's rescue of a boy in distress.

"My dancing with Charles Blake – oh, I do not seek attention and hope that such an unusual demonstration by a newcomer does not show me in that light."

"By no means. It was charming, but, remind me, how it came about that a young boy, unknown to you, should engage you for his first two dances?"

"He had been disappointed by Miss Osborne who, in engaging herself to an officer, reneged on her promise to young Charles. I was sitting nearby and merely offered to take her place."

"And in doing so you made the acquaintance of the entire Osborne family and their party without need of introduction or connection. How wonderful! There are many in the neighbourhood who have been attempting to attract their notice for years with little success."

"Not so Mr Tom Musgrave, by all appearances. He notices no other persons but the Osbornes and they cannot help but notice him, for he is everywhere at their elbows or about their feet."

"You do not like him?"

"I hardly know. He is certainly charming and animates any gathering that he is a party to but I feel that he would not promote any person's interest as much as his own."

"You are severe. He is greatly liked by all the young ladies."

"Although not so much by their mothers, perhaps." At this, Miss Edwards laughed and Emma laughed with her.

The sound of a bell announced the arrival of a visitor. Before Miss Edwards had time to summon her mother, the door was opened by a maid who stepped to one side and, as she was announcing their visitor, Tom Musgrave bounded in with a look of surprise at finding only the two young ladies within.

Both girls coloured, astonished at his sudden and unexpected appearance, for their commentary on him still hung in the air. He took their colour as a compliment to himself and as Miss Edwards asked the maid to beckon her mother from the library, he apologised for the suddenness of his visit.

"I had seen you, Miss Watson, pull up in your carriage earlier and wished to ask most particularly after your father's health."

"He is well, thank you."

Emma's response was short. Tom Musgrave had no interest in her father's health, of this she was convinced. Instead, he was throwing himself in her way again that he might strengthen their acquaintance, extract information from her and relate particulars back to Lord Osborne. Miss Edwards, anticipating a cool reception of their guest from her mother, resolved to sit in silence until the latter joined them. The lack of encouragement from the ladies did not dishearten Tom Musgrave in the least, and he took the liberty of positioning himself by the mantelpiece. With one elbow on the mantel and the other on his hip, Tom continued his cheerful musings aloud, wondering how they found the weather and whether there was any way he could be of assistance at Stanton.

"I abhor idleness, you must know. It is always the way with me to ask, when I enter a room, 'How may I be of service?'

and so, Miss Watson, with your father so indisposed, rest assured that you may call on me at any time."

Emma nodded her thanks.

"I believe I must congratulate the Watson family on the most advantageous marriage of your sister Penelope to a Dr Harding of Chichester."

"Thank you, sir, on behalf of my family. We are pleased that she is so happy in her new situation."

"She comes to visit you soon, I understand."

"Why, yes, she does." Emma wished to know how he knew but thought it impertinent to ask.

"And with a party, I believe."

"Yes, with her husband and his niece and nephew, Mr and Miss Shaw. They include a visit to family outside Dorking during their stay." She bit her lip when she saw his eagerness to hear and added, "I beg your pardon, Mr Musgrave, but how came you to know this?"

"Indeed, I did not know it. I heard a little at the White Hart, where I reside. The rest you have just informed me." A look of complacency crossed his face.

Emma's colour rose again for she had been tricked into saying more than she had wished. Just then, Mrs Edwards rushed into the room.

"This is quite improper, Mr Musgrave, for you to call unexpectedly like this. Had I known you were to honour us with a visit, I should not have left the young ladies unchaperoned in your presence. Why, this is how Miss Thornton came to ruination – two unsupervised meetings and an elopement. It is highly improper of you, sir, and you should have turned on your heels when you saw that a parent was not present. These casual comings and goings, at any hour of the day, may be all the fashion now but I would much rather advance notice."

"Madam, I had the most urgent enquiry to make of Miss Watson, on behalf of Lord Osborne. I am sure you would not intend any disrespect to his lordship. He had visited Mr Watson himself only very recently and with great concern for his welfare requested of me that if I chanced to spy any of the Miss Watsons about town, I was to find them out and make most intimate enquiries after their father's health. Such was my commission of sorts."

Mrs Edwards was clearly taken aback at the sheer audacity of this young man's willingness to talk nonsense to her, in her own home.

"Sir, please pass on my best regards to Lord Osborne and all his family and kindly inform him that I would not wish him to live in such agitated suspense with regards the health of any of his neighbours. As Mr Watson is a dear old friend of my husband's, we make enquiries of his health every other day. Please inform his lordship that, if he wishes it, I will happily send a note to the castle, containing Mr Watson's current state of health as soon as it is known to me. He may, therefore, sleep soundly at night and without the need to have his friend scrambling about town in the hope of happening upon unsuspecting, respectable ladies in an attempt to extract information from them."

Emma, sitting on one side of the fireplace, enjoyed a side view of Tom Musgrave and concentrated very hard to keep her face from betraying any reaction to what she heard. Mrs Edwards' speech was committed to memory so she might retell it to Elizabeth when home. She would also have to relate how Tom Musgrave's face contorted, how it was his turn to change colour and how quickly he withdrew from the room on its conclusion. He uttered apologies but he really had to be elsewhere on important business and so forth, hoping that he might see Mr Edwards at the hunt etc. and speedily left their company.

On her journey home to Stanton, Emma recalled with awe the confidence of Mrs Edwards and how she had spoken so frankly and stood up to an obvious rogue without coarseness. She had cleverly exposed his unpleasing exaggerations and insincere flatteries while assuming the role of protector. Emma contemplated how fortunate Miss Edwards was to have such a parent who, although firm, was caring and mindful of her daughter. She felt a sudden pang of yearning for her own Aunt Turner and mourned the absence of loving guidance she had assumed would be hers on reaching the age of balls and courtship. She wrote to her aunt, of course, but knew that those letters did not reveal all that would have been confided in person. How she longed to tell her aunt all the particulars of new acquaintances formed since her return to Stanton – some pleasing, others less so. Most of all, she wished to know what her aunt would think of Mr Howard. Would she find him amiable; approve of his manners and livelihood? Would she join in Emma's excitement when discussing him and make her blush by teasing her often? And most importantly – would her aunt see him, as Emma now did (despite having met him on only one evening and danced two dances with him) as the most likely gentleman of her acquaintance to secure her future happiness?

CHAPTER EIGHT

O n the day prior to Penelope's visit, the sisters
received an invitation from the Edwardses to stay
with them while attending the ball in Dorking in
two days' time. They did not have time to discuss which of the
sisters would attend this – although Margaret immediately
made it known that she simply *must*. In the same morning,
Elizabeth also received a letter from Mrs Ellingham, the
widow of a cousin with whom Mr Watson had grown up.
Though Mrs Ellingham lived but twenty miles away, she
had not visited the Watsons since Mrs Watson had passed
away all those years ago. Her only son, Harold, had recently
gone to sea and so on hearing that Mr Watson's health had
worsened, she had the inclination to finally make the visit.
Elizabeth consulted her father, who was delighted at the
prospect of reuniting with an old friend, remembering her
to be a warm, loquacious lady, and as the spare room was
not in use, a letter containing their delight in receiving her
was dispatched at once.

Penelope and her new husband arrived earlier than
expected the following morning, just as Elizabeth had gone
to tend to her father. As their coach approached the house,

it was left to the other two sisters to greet them.

"How very like Penelope to arrive early and catch us off guard," said Margaret.

At the door, Margaret stepped forward to greet the carriage as it pulled up with a welcome of sighs and fussing. She was "quite overwhelmed" to be reunited with her "beloved sister who looked so well, not at all freckly as before". The doctor was very welcome to their humble abode. A family could never have enough doctors among them. Did he treat back pain, for she was suffering greatly, with tending to their father?

Despite wearing a bergere over her cap to denote her changed status, Penelope looked much younger than Emma had expected. The doctor, by contrast, resembled one of their father's many acquaintances. There was carelessness about his appearance and proportions that made one think he had been a confirmed bachelor and had given up all thought of marriage but was caught now, suddenly and unawares, with a wife. A broad smile, however, revealed that he was content with his lot and pleased to widen his connections at this hour of his life.

Penelope now commenced speaking, with more vivacity than Margaret but less performance,

"Why, this must be Emma! Henry, let me introduce you to my youngest sister. Emma, this is my husband, Dr Harding."

"I am very pleased to meet you, Miss," the doctor said shaking her hand. She knew him then, from the warmth of his handshake, to be a most agreeable and genuine man and his sincerity further lessened her fear of his wife, who had already moved into the house but could still be heard without. The others followed her lead and soon they were all sitting together in the drawing-room where tea was to be served before daughter and father were reunited.

"You will love the Shaws," Penelope said. "John Shaw is perhaps peculiar but his sister more than makes up for it."

Dr Harding attempted to explain: "He is an expert in zoology, my dear, takes him all over the ..."

"But he is very good at cards and can always be relied upon to make up a table when we are short. And his sister is the most charming girl in the world. They are neither of them married or engaged."

"Oh, what a fine thing for Emma and Elizabeth," said Margaret, getting up and moving to the window seat, looking dreamily through the glass. "I, however, shan't be paying him any attention."

"No, oh, dear me, no! I would not recommend him for any of you," answered Penelope. "You will understand when you meet him, but otherwise they are a delightful family and Louisa has the most exquisite collection of fans that you ever did see. Does she not, my dear?"

Dr Harding started, having retreated to his own thoughts for a moment. He had not expected to be consulted on fans and dispatched a quick "Absolutely, absolutely" before turning his attention to the view from the window at the side of the house.

"That is as handsome a field as ever I saw."

"Indeed," continued Penelope, "you three are fortunate to meet with the Shaws for I attempted to dissuade them from joining us. What could be of interest to them here, when they could have been to Bath in the same time? There was really no need, as I told them, to make any effort to acquaint themselves with my family. John cared not a jot where he laid his head for a few weeks but Louisa insisted, wishing to pay a compliment to myself and also to meet their elderly relatives outside Dorking. Perhaps she is cunning and is in for an inheritance. I had almost convinced John but his sister was adamant so he had to give way."

All sisters and husband smiled, comment neither sought nor welcome during Penelope's speech.

At last Margaret sighed and said, "I shall show every interest in your friends, Penelope, that is within my power to do so but, you know, my attentions are often sought in another quarter."

Penelope stared, then said, "Good Lord, you are not still stuck on Tom Musgrave. He cares naught for you."

Margaret's colour changed and for a few moments Emma was unable to decipher which direction her fury and humiliation would take – a verbal retaliation, regardless of the stranger in their midst, or a storming from the room in hysterical tears. Margaret chose the latter. Elizabeth, descending the stairs to meet the guests, was almost knocked over by her retreating sister but, accustomed to such outbursts, she joined the company with her congratulations and was not curious in the least to know what ailed Margaret.

At last, Penelope declared they had best meet with her father that they might return to Dorking where they were engaged to spend the evening with the Shaws. Ten minutes upstairs and they were done. Returning to the room,

Penelope announced, "I wish Father would allow us to rid his room of all those things he gathers. It is in such disarray, I could hardly move without overturning something. And then he apologised to my husband that he had not more to leave his daughters. I was quite ashamed. What is the point in speaking of it now?"

Waving her gloves, Penelope continued, "More importantly, let me tell you that we will see you all on Saturday evening, dear sisters. I have convinced papa that his friend Mrs Ellingham will be here to tend to him, so that you may all attend the ball."

"Thank you, Penelope, but Mrs Ellingham could not possibly be asked to undertake such a duty, on the very day after her arrival. She is our guest, not hired help. We do not know how her own health is – she may be frail or nervous," replied Elizabeth.

"Not so frail and nervous that she cannot easily travel twenty miles of bad roads in winter. Father has agreed to the scheme, at my particular request. If Mrs Ellingham should need to call for help, James and Nanny are about and Betty is here to cook breakfast."

Emma secretly delighted in the plan, for she never expected to attend a ball with all three of her sisters. How clever Penelope now appeared in her eyes, to execute such a scheme and, therefore, it was with a tighter hug that she bade her farewell than had earlier greeted her.

Friday brought a short, stout lady with a kind and good-humoured face. Mrs Ellingham had in her life mothered more than the one son she had borne. As a younger woman, she had often taken in other children whose families fell on hard times through illness or death. Now she threw her arms around the girls as though known to her all their lives. Her enquiries as to the whereabouts and circumstances of their siblings reflected a genuine interest in the welfare of the family. She had heard a rumour with regards Mr Watson's health and felt a visit must not be put off until the spring. Her first meeting with him was emotional for all who were present. The two delighted in meeting again after such a long separation and tears were shed for loved ones now gone. They were then left alone to discuss the intervening years – their blessings and woes – and to find comfort in a sympathetic ear.

Later that afternoon, Mrs Ellingham mentioned the ball and insisted that she stay with Mr Watson, that he might delight in knowing that all his daughters attended the dance together. A small dispute arose – refusals and insistences, until finally the older generation won out, leaving the girls to commence planning in earnest. A note was dispatched at once to the Edwardses to inform them that their kind invitation to stay on the morrow would be accepted with gratitude by all three sisters living at Stanton.

Preparations for the ball began early the following morning. Anxiety to look well and command Tom Musgrave's attention put Margaret quite out of sorts. Her curls would not comply, her shoes were missing and there was a small stain on the dress she had set her heart on wearing.

"She retired to bed an angel and has awoken as a weasel!" Elizabeth confided in Emma when alone. "She possesses many qualities but good humour is not one of them. For my part, I pity the man who takes her – his misery is guaranteed.

It would be as well for him to get a good thrashing every day and be done with it, than to put up with such a woman."

"And yet marriage is the only route she may take?"

"Yes. Single women have a dreadful propensity for being poor – which is one very strong argument in favour of matrimony. She must marry and I pray that it will happen soon," said Elizabeth, "that she may rob a gentleman of his fortune and us of her company."

CHAPTER NINE

On the afternoon of the ball, Emma was delighted to receive a letter from her Aunt Turner, now O'Brien, and rushed to her bedroom to read it. Following greetings, enquiries after her health and that of the family, the most pressing matters at hand were arrived at.

... We are to sell Claperton Park ... The current tenants have given their notice and my husband does not believe it practical for us to manage matters from such a distance as Ireland. He is right, I dare say. Can you imagine it, Emma, your home and mine to be forever lived in by strangers? It saddens me but the Captain is quite determined. We are here now, at Claperton, to oversee the dispatch of items of value and importance and to meet with the agent to discuss all particulars. I did request that you could be sent for, that you should keep me company for these few weeks, but he felt it would be a tiresome and melancholic business for you. He means it kindly, Emma, for he sees how upset I have become and does not wish to further aggravate my nerves. I will write again soon, my dear, you are

ever in my thoughts ...

Such a shock as this could only meet with tears and since she was now safe, in the privacy of her bedroom, they had their way. Much as she had come to accept that Stanton was now her permanent home, there was still, within her heart, a dash of hope that her aunt and Captain O'Brien might yet return to Claperton Park and summon her to join them. All such expectations were now gone. In the immediate shock, it felt as though she had forever lost her home, her beloved aunt and any hope of future security. When the tears were run out, Emma went to find Elizabeth and give her a report of their aunt.

There was no surprise in how Elizabeth received the news and how she demonstrated a practical application of kindness – a quick hug dispensed and a sympathetic smile accompanied by a "Now, now, Emma, dry your tears. I thank God every day that you have been returned to me, selfish creature that I am. Come now, we must dress for the ball. The Edwardses' carriage will arrive soon."

There are few whose spirits do not improve during the excitement of readying oneself for a ball and Emma, even under such a disappointment, was no exception. The sisters ran from room to room, chattering, laughing and assisting each other in appearing their finest. Once returned to a happier disposition, Emma looked in upon her father and found Mrs Ellingham quite at home in a low chair, wearing spectacles and reading aloud from a book.

"And now, Mr Watson, I will retire for a while to return to you later and finish this chapter."

"Thank you, Mrs Ellingham," he replied. "You have been very kind."

Placing a wick in the book to mark her page, Mrs Ellingham smiled at Emma before leaving the room and gently closing the door after her.

When he was sure that he heard her footsteps descending the stairs, Mr Watson began, "Really Emma I do not know how you expect me to tolerate this woman! Is there any way to banish her from our home?"

"Father! It is only her second day. We believed you enjoyed her company. Has she been unkind?"

"Not unkind, if reading these dreadful novels is not considered unkind. I dislike them intensely. I had much rather be forever alone than in the company of a very bad book."

Emma, relieved, laughed. "You must tell her, Father, and do so thoughtfully."

"I did attempt to encourage her to read something from my own library but she found them dull and kept nodding off. So I have spent the past several hours in agony – hours that I have not to spare at this time of my life."

"This would greatly injure her feelings. She has given her time to come here and cheer you," said Emma, while moving about the room, pushing back chairs and taking books from his bedside and placing them back on the bookshelf.

"And what of my time? Recall, my dear, what Shakespeare said: '*I wasted Time and now doth Time waste me.*' But, yes, yes, she is a kind and attentive old friend. And that being so, I had best find another way. I have been thinking, if I feel a little stronger tomorrow, I will come downstairs. In company, I should be safe. She will have no need to read to me. Yes, that is what I will do. I will listen to this hogwash this evening, while you are all at the ball, and tomorrow afternoon, when you have returned, I will declare myself well enough to join you for dinner."

"Father, such a scheme!"

"Illness is a dangerous indulgence at my time of life. My poor cousin! I no longer wonder at his moving onto his heavenly home at such a young age. The miracle is that he did not depart sooner."

"I shall go now," said Emma with a laugh, kissing him on his forehead, "and leave you to your fate."

"Yes, you girls must go and enjoy your ball. I pray there will be a sufficient number of wealthy gentlemen who, in falling for your beauty, will kindly overlook your careless father's inability to provide you with a dowry. You may tell me all on the morrow."

Emma hesitated outside the closed door and sought to hear that noise which she had recently detected on leaving her father. It was the creaking noise of her father alighting from his bed, then moments later another creaking sound as he returned to it. She had learned that he regularly sought comfort from the log book which Emma had just now returned to the bookshelf. From his bed, she assumed, he would read with pleasure those entries which logged all his parish duties over thirty-three years and would be found later, lying on his coverlet, while he slept. Smiling at his mischievousness, Emma descended the stairs cheerier than when she had ascended it earlier and waited for the

Edwardses' carriage to arrive.

Later that evening, in the company of the Edwards family, the Watson sisters entered the assembly-room at Dorking to hear, among the general giddiness, that the Osborne set had already arrived. Their being first instead of last had never occurred in the history of Dorking, nor in the history of Tom Musgrave, who had found himself very much caught unawares – unprepared and undressed. Emma Watson had only time for one quick glance along the bustling room before spying Lord Osborne moving directly towards her. Having decided it a perfect evening to undertake his maiden dance in public he requested the pleasure of the first two dances and was gone to the orchestra to call the dance. In his brief absence, Penelope, beneath a showy headpiece of peacock feathers, waved to summon her sisters and offered her seat by the fire to Mrs Edwards, that she might stand by her husband and begin her introduction of the Shaws.

The manner of this meeting did not transpire as Elizabeth Watson had imagined. In passing along the brilliantly lit room, hers were visions of pleasant flirtations, an admiring glance from Mr Shaw and a request for the honour of dancing with her. Instead, she was greeted with cool indifference. On Penelope introducing her sister, he gave an abrupt, short bow, scant look and turned his back to continue his conversation with his uncle, Dr Harding.

A short bustle ensued, as gentlemen stepped forward to claim the hands of those to whom they were engaged. It was while Margaret and Miss Edwards danced with the officers, and all eyes were on Emma and Lord Osborne, that Penelope commenced her observations:

"Now there Louisa, my sister has been singled out and is dancing with a lord. We will be dining at Osborne Castle yet."

Miss Louisa Shaw, a pretty, reserved girl of three and twenty, replied, "Indeed you may but I believed she had only recently returned to Stanton, their courtship must be a new departure."

"That appears to be irrelevant, my dear," intervened Mr Shaw who at this stage returned to join the general conversation, apparently on purpose to entertain. "Once a man has a castle, ladies imagine themselves admiring the view from a turret by the end of their first meeting."

"You mistake my sister's character, Mr Shaw," Elizabeth responded quickly. "She has not the mercenary tendencies that some young ladies possess or are forced into. Emma has greater expectations of the wedded state and will certainly not rush into it, unless her happiness is assured."

"Oh John, you are in trouble." His sister laughed good-naturedly.

After a pause, Mr Shaw said, "I beg your pardon, Miss Watson. If your sister has high expectations then I have been presumptuous. I spoke generally, perhaps, but also from experience."

"As a single man, I give you leave to be an expert in marriage but as to the nature and inclinations of my sister, I allow myself to be the greater expert between us two."

"I stand corrected. I am no expert in marriage. I have often declared that I would rather be tied by the ankles and dragged about a muddy field by ten oxen than take a wife. I enjoy my freedom, you see. Why should I give up the admiration of many for the criticism of one?"

He made his comments for the amusement of the group and was rewarded with their laughter.

"Why indeed?" replied Elizabeth, after politely waiting for the merriment to ease. "The admiring masses must be such that I expect a stampede at any moment."

Just then they were joined by Solomon Tomlinson who requested of Mrs Edwards an introduction to the entire party. He had earlier judged the Shaws to be people of fashion and means and so, once introductions were made, immediately struck up conversation with Miss Shaw, culminating in a request to partner with her for the next two dances.

Before she had a moment to respond, her brother, who likewise had been observing Mr Tomlinson and having heard him talked of at the inn, had formed his own judgements and spoke: "I fear not, sir, for she has promised me these next two and is then engaged with one of the officers. I am afraid it will then be time for tea and we must retire early for I have plans for a trip tomorrow morning. Here, however, is Miss Elizabeth Watson, whom I am sure you are acquainted with. Let me present her to you, as a very pleasant substitute."

Elizabeth's tongue deserted her by such a humiliating turn of events and as Mr Tomlinson hesitated, obviously dissatisfied with the necessity of wasting the next two dances with a lady he had no intention of encouraging, her mortification deepened. Finally deciding that rejecting Mr Shaw's suggestion might displease the man whose good opinion he was attempting to court, Mr Tomlinson escorted Elizabeth to the floor, with Mr Shaw and his sister following suit. That Mr Tomlinson found dancing with her a chore and spoke not a word for the entire half hour satisfied Elizabeth for it left her free to dwell uninterrupted on thoughts of a most vile nature. Mr Shaw's self-congratulatory smile of amusement, which Elizabeth spied as she danced down the couples, only added to her silent vow to punish his despicable behaviour. The only other smile she met with, while dancing, came from Emma. It was a more sympathetic smile and a response to Elizabeth rolling her eyes heavenward. By the dance's end, Elizabeth had confirmed to herself that while he might dress like a gentleman, Mr Shaw was the most ill-bred man in England.

Emma, meanwhile, was painfully engaged with Lord Osborne. His dancing was true to his personality, as was their conversation – all awkwardness and oddities, leaving her to wonder why he would put himself through something so dreadful. She did acknowledge to herself, however, his openness in confessing, early in the dance, that he hated crowds and felt more comfortable among his own set. This she felt was an awareness of his own social ineptitude and, taking it as a sign to turn the subject to one which would put him more at ease, she enquired into his passion for outdoor pursuits. The effect was immediate. He was quite a different man and spoke with fluency on the topic, providing details of horses, rifles and hounds, about which she knew nothing. His relief, however, at touching on a home subject, gave her respite at last – anything was better than the agonising tension and silences of before, which might wrongfully be viewed by some keen observers (for there were many) as the natural shyness that accompanies the early stages of courtship.

"You must come to Stanton Woods when we take off from there on Tuesday the eighth. Fresh air and a purposeful task – what else is there to it?"

"I thank you but we may be engaged with the Shaws and my sister then. I believe they have some plans while they are hereabouts."

"And when are they to return home to Chichester?"

Emma remained silent.

"Then I shall speak to them all directly the dance is over and invite them too. In fact, I believe my mother mentioned something about arranging a special breakfast party on the morning of the hunt. You must all come."

Though Emma did not dislike Lord Osborne, he had about him the manner of a child who always got his way. She disapproved of the bullish manner in which he jumped into every undertaking, confident of success. When he wanted something, she doubted not, it was his for the taking, but she feared that in this instance he saw that "something" as herself.

When he accompanied Emma back to her group, they were all just returned from dancing likewise. When introductions were complete, Tom Musgrave burst upon them, only now ready and dressed – stating his disappointment at not being with them sooner. Lord Osborne got straight to the matter in hand.

"We set out hunting Tuesday the eighth from Stanton Woods. You are all to come to a breakfast party at the castle. Lady Osborne will send invites."

The directness of his manner rendered the group momentarily silent – unsure as to how best to respond. Mr Shaw, at last, offered a reply: "I fear you may have approached the wrong company, sir, there are not many among us equipped for such an undertaking. We have not a horse between us."

Tom Musgrave recognised his opportunity to be of service. "I am sure what his lordship refers to is that we must make a social occasion of it. The breakfast party to see the riders off. Is this not so?"

"Yes, exactly. That is it. We must meet and I will show you my horses and dogs. There, it is settled."

"Yes, of course," said Margaret, directing her words to Tom Musgrave. "I am delighted you asked."

Lord Osborne said a satisfied "Good evening" to the party, and turning to Emma added, "Good evening, Miss Watson." Then, the purpose of his joining them done, he set off to the card-room. Tom Musgrave bowed and made after him, only looking back to confirm the astonishment of the ladies, an outcome which seemed to delight him.

It was a wonderful thing, declared Elizabeth, who loved how their life was getting ever more exciting daily. The only unfortunate occurrence was that Mr Tomlinson was still of the party when the invite was issued and, therefore, included himself in the plans. As he left the group shortly after, he gave Louisa Shaw a meaningful glance, observed by all present, that she might know she had been singled out as his particular favourite.

"Mr Shaw," said Elizabeth, turning to the gentleman next to her, swilling his glass, "you have only arrived in Dorking yet I believe both you and your sister have already earned the admiration and deep regard of Solomon Tomlinson."

"Deep, you say? I cannot imagine anything runs deep with that gentleman. If he is an example of the specimen of person we are to meet hereabouts, we may have to cut our trip short."

"Do not be so quick to judge the local population, I beg you. We are not all blessed with Mr Tomlinson's wit and charm."

"I am very glad to hear it but I tend to form my own opinions. Few reach my standard of good company."

"I can imagine, Mr Shaw, you have a great many friends."

"Yes, many."

"'Many' is a very common word, used all too freely these days, I find."

"I shall report back at the end of my stay, if you wish, and inform you whether the people of Dorking and its surrounding countryside reach my standards. Early indications are not looking favourable."

"Indeed! I'm sorry to hear it," said Elizabeth, now quite out of patience with his arrogance, "especially as early indications would also point to your sister perhaps becoming a local resident in time. I do hope her standards are not as exacting as yours for I would very much like to call on her. Did you happen to see the Tomlinsons' manor as you approached the town?"

Mr Shaw frowned but did not answer and what followed was a long silence between the two, broken only by the approach of Dr Harding whose generous praise of the evening livened up the sullen pair.

Soon the four sisters were chatting happily together at tea. All were pleased in their own way – Emma as her next dance was with Mr Howard, Margaret as she believed that Tom Musgrave had contrived the breakfast party for her benefit, and Penelope because she had a wealthy husband to parade in front of former neighbours; Elizabeth, perhaps, was the happiest of all, for not having attended a ball for twelve months, she had come with the express intention of making up for lost time. And once Mr Shaw sat down to the card-table and could be forgotten about, she finished out the night laughing heartily and dancing every dance.

When the music started up again, Mr Howard came to claim Emma's hand and she was struck at once with the warmth that shone through his eyes. How did their animation escape her on their first meeting, for now it was all she could see – they were positively smiling at her.

As they danced, Mr Howard enquired of Emma, "What, may I ask, do you think of my curate, Mr Tomlinson?"

She smiled. "I cannot say."

"Surely you can. Speak now, what do you think of his character?"

"I cannot speak so freely, regardless of what I think. A woman's opinions are not always genuinely sought … and when given frankly are regarded as coarse and reflect worse on her own character than on the individual about whom she is commenting."

"I assure you that is not the case here. I do not hold what is spoken as truth and with honesty, in contempt. So speak, if you please."

"I cannot."

"You have a tongue in your head, I believe, and a mind of your own? Surely you have read Wollstonecraft – she is widely available in all the circulating libraries."

"I do find him a little peculiar but perhaps on knowing him more, I will understand him better."

Mr Howard smiled and said, "Perhaps."

They laughed conspiratorially.

"Unfortunately, however, he is somewhat out of sorts with me at present," said Mr Howard.

"How so?" Emma had asked it when she had only meant to think it, but Mr Howard seemed amused at her curiosity and continued,

"He had heard that I was offered the living at Branchfield, which is true. It would give me a suitable house nearby for my sister while it is well within my capacity to manage the extra duties in addition to Wickstead. Mr Tomlinson, however, believes I should vacate Wickstead and encourage Lady Osborne to offer it to him."

"So very bold. Why would he do such a thing?"

"He is anxious to attain a living as soon as possible, that his climb upwards may begin. I fear he was bitterly disappointed with the response he received. As a man born with a natural sense of entitlement, however, I feel he will not remain dejected for long."

Mr Howard then asked Emma how her days were spent and what her favourite pursuits were. She owned that she had less now since her return to Stanton but she kept up her daily walks and enjoyed drawing. He in turn revealed himself as an amateur astronomer, an unusual pastime for a clergyman and one, he claimed, that often extracted laughter from others. Emma, however, thought it delightful and as the music ceased, sensed a natural understanding arise between them. They joined Mrs Blake, who approached them from the tea-room, and all three sat down. After inquiries about Charles were met with a favourable response, Mrs Blake noted her difficulty in encouraging him to comply with his studies rather than spend all his time at the stables at Osborne Castle.

"And I do so wish he would learn languages for he may wish to travel, as his father had done before him, but I cannot find a tutor."

"I would be happy to teach him French and Italian, if you wish. Certainly, for the coming month or so at least, while there are many women in the house, I will be at liberty more often than knowing what to do with my time and I should like to be useful."

Mr Howard and his sister were all amazement, saying that they could not accept such a generous offer, but Emma smiled and insisted. Wickstead was but two miles from Stanton. She walked every day, so why not with a purpose? It might only be for a short time, while they had additional company, and the teacher would benefit far more than the pupil by teaching those languages which she loved, but had never had the opportunity to use until now.

"Then it is settled," said Mr Howard, smiling warmly. "We cannot thank you enough. Come whichever day you find yourself free to do so."

All Emma heard or saw for the remainder of the evening was coloured by the joyful expectancy that the forthcoming adventure provided; and sensing the relief it had brought

Mrs Blake and her brother, she delighted in the scheme all the more. Back at the Edwardses' home, all aspects of another marvellous ball were discussed over soup and no person that evening escaped a kind word from Emma. Even Solomon Tomlinson was deemed "less irksome" than she had expected and was commended for wearing a most delightfully large cravat.

CHAPTER TEN

On the second day following the ball, and
after only very little teasing from her sisters,
Emma made her first trip to Wickstead. As she
approached along the beech-lined sweep to the house,
she was surprised to find it a grand glebe parsonage with
what looked like a walled garden to one side and well-
maintained out-buildings to the other. It was much finer
than Stanton and larger, for the fields which surrounded
it, she supposed, must also belong to the rectory. That Mr
Howard stood in great favour with the family at the castle
was now apparent, for to receive the living of Wickstead
and maintain the property and the staff numbers required
to manage it must be a generous living. The turrets of the
castle itself were just visible over a copse of oaks beyond the
field leading from the out-buildings, a constant reminder
of where gratitude was owed.

Mrs Blake met Emma with warmth and appreciation
while Charles jumped up and down beside her. Just as they
moved from the door, a woman and child were leaving it.
Mrs Blake explained: "Please excuse all the coming and
going, Miss Watson. My brother receives persons to his

study regularly, to seek advice or to put in a good word at the castle. This is a busy household."

To Charles's consternation, they moved first into the parlour for tea and Emma declared it to be the sweetest room she had ever seen – neat, sparsely furnished yet elegant, with freshly cut flowers and such feminine touches as reflected Mrs Blake's influence and excellent taste. Mrs Blake enquired after her father and sisters and repeated how very obliged she was to her for her great kindness and how convinced she was they would become the best of friends. With a smile, Mrs Blake added, "But we already hold you in the highest regard here, Emma, and have done so since our first meeting. My brother and I are so glad that we have come to know you; we often say so."

When finished with tea, Mrs Blake insisted that she walk Emma through the principal rooms so that she might feel at home at Wickstead. During this tour of the house she met with Charles's younger siblings in the playroom and later Mr Howard in his study. He welcomed the ladies and Charles in and appeared keen to delay them from their purpose by asking many questions regarding the weather, conditions of roads and general likelihood of rain. Emma was reminded of her late uncle and his private study at Claperton Park as she looked around at the book shelves, compasses, globe and other tools of matriculation; she smiled on spotting a telescope by the window.

"Ah, you see, I was not telling a lie. I am the clergyman astronomer – the rare man who believes in God and Science. This is the best window from which to observe the night sky with no trees or castles to obscure my view.

Do you find me quite mad yet, Miss Watson?"

"On the contrary, sir, your admiration of the stars is a tribute to nature and I am all for nature. In fact, my uncle presented me with a map of the stars of the southern hemisphere once. It is one of the only mementos I have from him and so it is very dear to me. I would be happy to let you look upon it. I could lend it to you."

He smiled, apparently pleased with her response. "I will interrupt you ladies and gent no longer. I see Charles is anxious to have you all to himself. Pray, do not let him talk of horses to you or your lesson is doomed before it begins. What time, Miss Watson, do you expect to finish? I will walk with you back to Stanton. There is an elderly lady, a former parishioner of mine, who has moved to live with her daughter near there, whom I would like to visit."

"I do not know. I may be lenient on Charles for our first lesson. One hour perhaps."

"Good, well, knock here on this door and I will be glad to accompany you home."

Emma delighted in everything that followed despite her impatience for the walk back to Stanton. Charles was a spirited but bright boy who fought between his desire to please his new teacher and his wish to be up and out of his chair at every noise outside. One moment it was a robin landing on the windowsill, next it was the gardener moving past with a barrow full of stones. The little, bright school room was evidently used by all the Blake children for four little desks sat side-by-side, with chalk boards on top. Mrs Blake had insisted that the others would not disturb their lesson and although they were curious about the pretty

Miss Watson, they were happy to comply if it meant they did not have to attend their lessons. A globe, similar to the one she noticed in Mr Howard's study, sat on a table at the top, which was to be her desk. Emma was so satisfied with Charles's progress and with her own ability to impart any instruction, a skill she had not realised she possessed, that at the hour's end, she glowed with contentedness and relief.

The lesson over, a nervous Emma knocked on Mr Howard's door, to find him hat in hand and enthusiastic for the excursion. They walked at a leisurely pace, conversing easily as Mr Howard, bearing a long stick, chopped the heads off unsuspecting roadside grass and weeds with a determined air. They had almost reached Stanton when Mr Howard said, "You must find it difficult – this unexpected change in your life."

"Yes, I must confess at times I do. But I count my blessings, am grateful for the love and kindness I have received, especially from my father and sister Elizabeth."

"Do they find you changed?"

"Very much so, but, then, I was not yet six years old when I left. I believe they perceive me as quite refined and I hope my manners do not offend them. I attempt to fit in to the ways at Stanton and occasionally must hide my shock at the manner in which matters are conducted. They should not and cannot change for me. It is for me to fit in. I have noticed that dear Mrs Ellingham has a very abrupt and unannounced manner of entering a room that makes me jump out of my seat. Then there is Elizabeth's frankness. Oh, forgive me, I do not mean to pass judgement. Elizabeth is a lady to her fingertips and the most affectionate creature I have ever met, it is only that I am still attempting to get used to her manner of speaking without reserve."

"Perhaps the necessity of becoming the mother of a large household when but a girl herself made her so. Perhaps she had to speak as she found, or risk losing the trust and respect of family, neighbours and tradespeople."

"Yes, I believe you are right. Elizabeth is practical, pleasant and open in all her ways. She has an ease, a simple belief that all will turn out well."

They had arrived at the door and were now facing each other smiling. Emma continued, "I now have the love of a sister that I had not known. When one thinks of all the truly important qualities in a sister – what of show, reserve and refinement? How can manners compare to goodness? What is etiquette to love?" Both ceased smiling and Emma looked away.

"What indeed?" said Mr Howard, but Emma found she could not face him and, feigning urgency, excused herself and was within, with her back pressed to the door, leaving the confused man without. It was several moments before she heard the stones crunch as he walked away – in what state of emotion, she knew not.

The subsequent days saw a gay party regularly gathered at Stanton. Even Mr Watson appeared frequently in their midst and in improved health. Emma congratulated Mrs Ellingham on contributing to this improvement.

"Indeed I find," said Mrs Ellingham, "that if you read to men who claim to be sick, very dreadful novels, there is a vast improvement in their health and mobility in a short period of time."

Emma stared in amazement. "Surely you have not been so cunning."

"Indeed I have. Men are such poor patients and they love to be fussed over. I do own that they are usually ill, in the extreme, when they take to their bed, but when the temptations are great to stay there, that is usually what they do. One must reverse the appeal and make them see that a drop of malt and some good conversation lifts their spirits and helps them to forget their aches and woes."

Emma smiled in agreement. There was certainly a great improvement in her father's mood but she could not deny that he was a very sick man, for whom Dr Richards held out little hope. Still, to see him in greater spirits, even though it might be for a short period, gave them all permission to be more at ease and enjoy themselves to a greater degree.

The Shaws, despite their grandeur, found Stanton cosy and full of charm, declaring themselves very much at home there. Mr Shaw, in particular, who was quite fond of cards, sat down many an evening as if he had no intention of leaving. Emma and Elizabeth also found in Penelope's husband such a pleasant, agreeable man that sometimes, just on meeting him, one could not help but be put in good form. Only Elizabeth and Mr Shaw did not get along. Their mutual dislike of each other was observed and, for the most part, largely ignored by the others present.

"Your father greatly enjoys Shakespeare," observed Mr Shaw to Emma. They had just witnessed a stream of soliloquys muttered from the losing Mr Watson, during a card-game, catching only the words "ill-fated", "chance" and "divinity".

"Yes, he is quite proficient," answered Emma.

"I dare say he often has cause to quote from *The Taming of the Shrew*," he responded while keeping his eyes fixed on Elizabeth.

Emma smiled. "Elizabeth is the sweetest creature, I assure you, Mr Shaw. You do not know her."

"Tell me, does she not treat all men with contempt? Or am I alone, the happy exception?"

Emma chose to sit close to the Shaws and found great enjoyment in their company. Elizabeth in avoiding Mr Shaw sat with her sisters – Margaret who spoke of nothing but the breakfast party at the castle and Penelope who encouraged her.

"It will be a great thing when Emma marries Lord Osborne for then we may treat the castle as quite our own," Penelope called out to the room in general.

"Do not say that, sister, please, I beg you. There is no understanding there, I assure you," Emma responded.

"Well there would be, if you did not avoid it. I saw you cross over to the milliner's in Dorking when you saw Tom Musgrave and Lord Osborne ride up to the White Hart. You were supposed to wait for me at the door."

"I did not wish to appear ..."

"Well, you should appear, whatever it was that you felt you should not. Do not worry, I have had a word with Tom Musgrave on your account."

"You waste your time, Pen," cried Margaret. "Emma cares only for Mr Howard. He walked her home from lessons with the boy the other afternoon and she daydreamed for the rest of the day."

"Well, either would do, I suppose – so long as he has a title and lives in a castle," Penelope finished with a laugh.

Emma sat quietly, looking into the fire. Elizabeth pressed a hand on her shoulder as she moved across the room to check on Mr Watson, otherwise all was still.

The short but strained pause was finally broken by Mr Shaw, who put a different slant on the conversation.

"Do not speak to me of suitors and attempted dalliances at inns. That dreadful Solomon Tomlinson has called to the White Hart on three separate occasions to divine our movements so that he might prey on my sister. What a nuisance he has become! There lives a tribe of cannibals in the Lesser Antilles to whom I would dearly love to introduce him."

"Oh, John, I am sure you misrepresent the man."

"No, I do not. I have it from the proprietor of the inn, who takes great pleasure in laughing at my vexation and mocks me with 'Imagine having Solomon Tomlinson as a brother-in-law. What a dreadful thing.' To which I say, 'Not as dreadful as having a Mr Shaw as a brother-in-law, I can assure you. Do you have a sister, perchance?'"

The general laughter put Emma a little more at ease and encouraged Mr Shaw to continue.

"Miss Tomlinson, however, is a pleasant young lady although her laugh sounds like three dozen suits of armour thrown down a staircase."

"I do not think Mr Tomlinson is as attentive to his sister's interests are you are, brother."

"I agree. What does he know of going about the country chaperoning his sister?"

"Oh John," said Louisa, amused.

"Well, John had much rather wake up in John's own bed. He had much rather sign over half of John's fortune to his dear sister and look at the view from his own window every morning instead of following her about the country and would do so, if John were not afraid that she might marry a fool."

"You give me no credit."

"My dear, had I known what one was contending with in Solomon Tomlinson, I would have marched you straight back to Chichester. Have pity on me, Louisa, at my age I hardly have the energy for hiding my sister in closets and wardrobes. Why, one moment of unsupervised conversation, with a little silliness or boredom on either side, and there we are at an engagement. Wedding bells and a honeymoon to the coast, before we know it."

He stood up and moved over to where Elizabeth was tidying away the tea items. Pouring and handing him the last remaining cup, Elizabeth said, "Tea, Mr Shaw? There is nothing like tea for comforting the soul and making social creatures of us all. There is nothing like tea for loosening the tongue."

"A complaint, I sincerely believe, Miss Elizabeth, which has never afflicted you in your entire life."

"It greatly depends on the topic, sir. You, for example, speak much of marriage for one who makes every effort to avoid it."

"Yes, it is much like sickness, rain and nuisance women,

in that regard; the more one tries to avoid them, the more one seems to attract. I must learn to speak less on the subject and perhaps then I shall have some peace."

"No, sir, please do no such thing. For then you might speak on more endearing subjects and appear in a better light. It would greatly upset me to find you all ease and pleasantries, for I have put great effort into forming my current opinion of you and it would upend all my work thus far. We would be a very dull party if each of us were full of niceties. You had best stay as you are."

"My word, Miss Watson, but you do enjoy giving me a taste of my own treatment of others. I shall endeavour not to disappoint you and will begin at once. This is the most dreadful tea I have ever tasted. It is too cold, too strong and too sweet."

"As was my intention, sir. Now if you will excuse me."

With that, Elizabeth handed Nanny, who had just entered the room, the tea things and moved back over to her sisters by the fire, with Mr Shaw following her movements all the while. Up to this point in his life, he had never met his equal for wit, openness and sarcastic social commentary and had ever looked down upon his company, wherever he went, as being far inferior to himself in its ability to observe and entertain. But here was the beautiful Elizabeth Watson – fearless in her approach and dumbfounding in her astuteness and though he had not admitted it to himself as yet, he was thoroughly captivated.

CHAPTER ELEVEN

I t was agreed among the sisters and Mrs Ellingham, who had extended her visit for another few weeks, that Tuesdays and Thursdays were Emma's days to teach Charles Blake. And without excuse or pretence, Mr Howard was found each day at the door of the school room just as the lesson was finishing, waiting to escort Emma home. As they left, he was often set upon by his little nephews and niece who chose different trees from which to jump and ambush him as he passed. Always feigning surprise, he defended himself heroically and begged for mercy but inevitably was defeated and, greatly humiliated, retreated at speed beyond the gate where he joined a laughing Emma.

She could not remember a happier time than those weeks walking between Wickstead and Stanton, in the company of Mr Howard. Their conversations were lively and varied and there was never an awkwardness or pause to overcome.

She told him of her favourite part of the walled garden at Claperton Park where her uncle had created a fairy corner of fern, heather, wildflowers, moss and ivy for her amusement. A small Persian-inspired pavilion building was commissioned for her pleasure, so she could spy on birds, butterflies and little fairy people in comfort. It was miniature in size so her aunt teased her, calling it 'the folly', while the gardener shook his head and looked perplexed every time he walked past it, yet it was her favourite place in the world.

Mr Howard told her how his interest in astronomy came about when as a boy he learned that the stars do not disappear when night passes but keep ablaze in the sky throughout the day. To him, such a miracle was greater evidence of cosmic intelligence, reassuring him that everything was held together and that he was never abandoned, never alone in the dark, and he professed his dream: "To live in awe of the universe and of use to man – is all that I wish for in this life. Well, perhaps, very nearly all that is to be wished for."

They discovered that they both had lost a parent when not yet ten years old and each acknowledged the immeasurable good fortune of being in the possession of a very loving sister.

Such confidences shared made Emma wish that the distance between their two houses was greater, for it always felt as though they were talking but minutes and, very often, when they arrived at Stanton, they continued talking still, at the door, unless the elements were against them. Kindred spirits, such as theirs, becoming more intimate in their sharing, saw no awkwardness, no thing to dislike. All that she mentioned to him was safe. She was safe and finally she came to know that "home" was not a place, but a feeling and a belonging.

On one of their walks to Stanton, Mr Howard began, "I wish to ask your opinion on something, Miss Watson, if I may?"

"By all means."

"I was considering moving my study to the rear of the house and perhaps converting my present study into a small sitting-room. The light is very good there. Would you advise it?"

"Oh! I see. Well, let me think this over. It is a very serious matter and one that deserves much deliberation. You read quite an amount in your study, sir, do you not?"

"Yes, Miss Watson, I do."

"I have seen your bureau and may suppose you write letters, sermons and documents – both of your business and ecumenical affairs, is it not so?"

"Yes, you are correct."

"The light in the study, as you have said, is very good and perhaps perfect for conducting these activities?"

"That is true."

"And all those who come to speak with you and seek your advice have only to take one or two steps from the front door and they are in your midst, which is most convenient."

"Very convenient."

"And have you not yourself declared the study window is a most advantageous point from which to admire the night sky with your telescope?"

"I confess it is so."

"Then you must convert your study at once into a sitting-room, in which nobody will sit and you and your telescope may move to the potting shed forthwith."

"Ha! We are of one mind, I see! ... In solemnity, however, the light at the rear of the house is very good in the mornings and that is when I conduct much of my business and writing. There exists a room upstairs, from which the view of the night sky is superior to anywhere else in the house and my hope is that another, in time, may desire to spend their time in a small, bright sitting-room with the best views of the surrounding countryside. Perhaps I might join them there on occasion."

His voice was faltering as he made the final remark and Emma felt there was nothing she could say. To change the subject would indicate a coldness and indifference to his intended meaning but a question would perhaps force him down a road he was not yet ready to go. She wished to encourage him but was unable to do so now, at this time and on a subject as suggestive as the one he had just presented. It would have to be for him to introduce his intentions with regard to his future and whether he saw her in it. If he wished to secure her affections, he could and would speak plainer, of this she was convinced. For now, she felt it best to do what she often did when presented with difficult choices – nothing at all. Mr Howard, aggressively beheading a bunch of nettles, soon turned the conversation back to safer topics until they reached Stanton and bid their goodbyes, each a little more self-conscious than before.

On the following Thursday, Emma found no Charles waiting for her in the school room. His mother, who was just then coming from the parlour, indicated that he must be yet with her brother and both ladies moved to the study to enquire. On entering when beckoned, Charles turned excitedly to Emma and asked, "What do you know of Venus, miss?"

Emma turned a deep crimson and responded, "Why, she is the Roman goddess of love, Charles; in mythology, of course."

She could not look at Mr Howard as she answered but was forced to do so, when he said, "I believe Charles was referring to the planet, Miss Watson, I was just showing him here through my telescope. Though it be daytime, we can make it out."

"Oh ... I did not ... how embarrassing."

"You were not to know. I would be happy to point planet Venus out to you. Please step up to the telescope. It is much easier to see now in the winter. It appears as the Evening Star, but it is, in fact, a planet. Please, come this way, if you will."

"Charles, come with me. I wish to speak to you about something most urgent," said Mrs Blake. "Now!"

Charles was reluctant to move, as he wished to give Emma the commentary he had just now himself received, but his mother's look brooked no argument so, with downcast face, he accompanied her from the room.

Mr Howard appeared shy and cleared his throat several times while Emma moved towards the telescope where he had just finished positioning it and looked through. Uneasy yet excited, she believed Mr Howard must surely hear her heart thumping, it beat so loud within her. After a few moments of adjusting the lens as he instructed her, she spotted Venus and spontaneously cried, "How amazing! How wonderful!"

She then asked Mr Howard, as the sky was clear and the moon was visible, if she could now look upon that. He repositioned the telescope slightly and again she stepped forward and looked in awe and wonder at the moon. How could something that she looked upon, almost daily, be so incredibly different and beautiful when seen in this way? Life, she informed Mr Howard, was so majestic and they both grinned and marvelled at seeing the celestial sky, as if newly born. A moment of awkwardness crept in, with neither person saying a word, until Emma's bonnet, which had been resting on an armchair, decided at this moment to fling itself to the floor. They both reached down but Mr Howard got there first and handed it to Emma.

"I think I hear Charles next door, commencing his lessons without me. I had best join him," said Emma.

"Of course."

"Thank you for showing me the heavens."

"Not at all. It was my pleasure. I would love to look upon the sky of the southern hemisphere someday. Who knows, it may come to pass."

"I will look out for my uncle's map, as I promised some time ago."

"Thank you."

"Goodbye."

"Goodbye, for an hour or so," and Mr Howard waved her off, as though she were departing for the Americas when she was merely moving to the next room and there was but a narrow wall between them.

That evening, Emma retired earlier than usual to the privacy of her bedroom where, lying on her bed and staring at the ceiling, she indulged in all the sweet imaginings of first love – replaying every word and tender look that she and Mr Howard had exchanged thus far. And when she dared think of the future, she smiled at how truly within her grasp those dreams felt. Though she was not the type of person to breathe a word of her expectations to another living soul, her heart could burst with the thought of soon letting everyone know that Mr Howard was her intended and she was his.

CHAPTER TWELVE

One afternoon, when her lesson was finished and Charles had run off to the castle, there was no Mr Howard waiting for Emma at the door. Distracting herself with corrections, she prolonged her stay for a few minutes before deciding to stop by his study on her way out, in case he had forgotten the time. As she approached, she heard voices within – the unmistakeable laugh of Lady Osborne responding to some amusing tale Mr Howard was telling. Emma felt a stab of pain, and, moving swiftly to the front door, let herself out. Her mind raced as she walked down the sweep, wondering at her lowness, and she muttered, "How silly of me, to feel jealous of his patroness calling upon him. She has every right and I have none." And yet a tear came to her eye and she wiped it away, taking deep breaths to calm herself. Then, just as she was passing through the gates, she heard her name called and she turned quickly to see Mr Howard waving and running towards her. He begged her pardon. He had lost track of time. Lady Osborne had called and they had parish matters to discuss.

They walked on in silence, Emma struggling to return

to her usual ease so he would suspect nothing of her recent feelings, but it was too late. Mr Howard began, "Ours is an unusual friendship, mine and Lady Osborne's."

Emma merely nodded. She wished to say "You do not need to tell me anything, it is no concern of mine" but she did not trust her voice, so he continued,

"I beg, Miss Watson, that you tell not a living soul what I am about to tell you, not even your sisters, for it was entrusted to me by one who suffered much in the telling. I will explain to you now of my connection with the castle and how I came to have the living. Lady Osborne, when unwed, was a young friend of my mother's – they wrote witty verse and plays together and laughed a great deal. She was a beautiful, carefree creature, thus popular wherever she went. She then captured the attention of Lord Osborne and theirs was a passionate courtship. He idolised her and she was infatuated with him. Once they were married, however, she lost her appeal in his eyes and his pettiness, cruelty and jealousy emerged. He controlled her every move – who she met, what she wrote and where she went. Over time, her anxiety increased. Nothing she did was right – she had yet to realise that you cannot please a man who would not be pleased. His son, he rejected. He was too attached to his mother. His daughter was his princess and everything that he had once lavished on his wife, he now lavished on the girl. It was around this time that I came to tutor the young master. My mother had offered my services, until such time as my studies at Oxford would commence. When I met Lady Osborne, she was no longer carefree and spirited as I had known my mother's friend to be. Her nerves troubled her greatly and she avoided company to escape his ridiculing her in public. I can see this upsets you, Miss Watson, I will say no more."

"It is a distressing history, but please, Mr Howard, continue."

"Very well, if you are quite sure. Lord Osborne was pleasant to me at first, interested in all I had to say, and took me under his wing. I must confess his character was so captivating that he did inspire a sort of loyalty in me, for there were many things I pretended not to see. The day came, however, when I could no longer ignore the excesses of his cruelty to his wife. I stayed his hand. At first, he looked on me in disbelief, but then the full force of his fury descended. His son was to be sent away to a harsh school in Birmingham. I too was to be gone, travelling with the boy as far as Oxford but no further. Lady Osborne was locked into her room for four days. Her only visitor was Lord Osborne. She was released on the morning we were setting off to say 'farewell' – a false act of kindness on the part of Lord Osborne, for he wished for us to see her in her lowest state. Words cannot describe what I witnessed that morning – her demeanour, her appearance and state of mind. What had he done? I believed I would not see her alive again – the woman before me would not live long – either by her own hand or someone else's – or she would end her days in an institution."

"Dear God! I cannot believe what I hear. This is the same Lady Osborne – so self-assured and poised. I beg your pardon for interrupting you."

"I was tormented with guilt. If I had not stayed his hand,

she would not be reduced thus. I wrote of my concerns to my mother. I hoped that perhaps we could find some former friends or relatives who would provide her with a safe home, if she could be convinced to leave. My mother was making preparations to this end when we heard, some weeks later, that Lord Osborne had died. He had caught a terrible fever and died at his mistress's home in London. On his deathbed, he sent an express to his wife, that she would come to him. She did not. Instead, she sent for the boy to be returned home."

Emma shook her head and Mr Howard continued, "This I tell you now, trusting you as I have not trusted another."

He stopped to look at her and she looked back, this time not hiding the tears that came freely to her eyes.

"I am so truly sorry. How much she has suffered, how much everyone involved has suffered. It is too much."

"But it is in the past now, thank Heavens. She is stronger and has made such changes to ensure the happiness of everyone under her care and patronage. She is a very good woman, to whom I owe a great deal."

Emma nodded. They strolled on in silence for much of the way, only stopping to chat on trivial subjects here and there. When Stanton was in sight, Mr Howard asked, "Will you be at Osborne Castle for the breakfast party next Tuesday?"

Up to this point, Emma had been convinced that it would be in her best interest to make her excuses and avoid the breakfast. She did not wish Lord Osborne to see her attendance as a compliment to himself but now Mr Howard's question gave her a fresh reason to go. With his eagerness in asking, coupled with a new sympathy for Lady Osborne and her son and the fact that Mrs Ellingham still remained at Stanton, she decided that the gathering might be an enjoyable one. She would attend but keep her distance from Lord Osborne. She expected it to be an extremely pleasant morning in the company of her sisters and friends, in particular Mr Howard and his sister. With a note of satisfaction and excitement in her voice, she informed Mr Howard, of her change of mind: "Yes, I will be there."

"Good. I look forward to it all the more now." They said their goodbyes, each with a heart and mind full to the brim of sorrow and hope.

CHAPTER THIRTEEN

On the morning of the breakfast party at Osborne Castle, Mrs Ellingham announced her departure from Stanton by the end of the week. Her son, Harold, was expected home on leave for Christmas and she wished to have their home ready for his arrival with all his favourite foods in the larder.

The sisters thanked her for her kindness and remarked on how often their father was downstairs enjoying company since she arrived.

"He is like a man ten years younger, Mrs Ellingham. You have restored his vigour."

"I cannot take all the credit, dear Elizabeth. The frequency and variety of the company you have at present, the mild weather, watching all his dear daughters together again and his love for my novels – all will have contributed."

Emma, in taking her father his breakfast that morning, reminded him that they were soon to set out for Osborne Castle and cajoled him regarding Mrs Ellingham's news.

"Father, you get your wish at last – Mrs Ellingham's departure."

"Yes, my dear, I am a man of faith but there were some

evenings, as she read, that I felt abandoned by my Maker. And yet, though it will be nice to have my quietude back, Mrs Ellingham was an excellent companion. I shall ... she will be missed at Stanton for she adds greatly to the happiness of any home, it would seem. By the by, I see the snowdrops have come up unnaturally early this winter due to the mildness. It is quite strange. Did I tell you that last week I noticed how that fine man, Mr Howard, was admiring my snowdrops?"

"Father! You were in bed the afternoon Mr Howard visited; how could you have seen him unless you were spying from this window?" Emma feigned surprise.

"Oh, yes, indeed, I was. Good fellow, he is. Likes flowers, I believe. Gives a marvellous sermon."

Emma shook her head as she left him in comfort to enjoy his breakfast and moved to her bedroom to begin dressing.

Elizabeth and Margaret did not have to ponder a great deal as to what they would wear to the castle for they must wear whatever was best, newest or had not yet been seen by those who would be in attendance. Emma alone, having brought many fine clothes and fabrics with her from Claperton Park, was not short of choice and offered freely to her sisters, but Elizabeth being taller and Margaret slimmer than she, they were unable to avail of the offer.

"My gowns are dreadful," announced Elizabeth as she descended the stairs to join her sisters for departure. "I am so tired and ashamed of my current stock that I blush at the sight of the wardrobe that contains them."

A note arrived just at that moment from Miss Edwards. Elizabeth read it aloud:

Dear friends, I fear I cannot join you this morning though I had wished it very much. I was all set for the journey and Anna had even taken in my light blue dress. My parents, however, have just now received an invite from the McDowells who are unexpectedly returned to Dorking and were loath to pass it up. They say I must join them, that it would be very bad for me not to see my cousins. They would not hear of me attending Osborne Castle without them. I am so very sorry. Do have a wonderful morning and come visit me, at your earliest convenience, that you may tell me all.

Your fond friend,
Mary Edwards

Despite this note and the disappointment they felt on behalf of its author, the sisters' excellent spirits could not be dampened for long. Emma, however, soon found a fresh worry and it embarrassed her to think how Elizabeth would laugh when she heard it. Her concern was whether it would appear very common to arrive at the castle with one of the three ladies driving the carriage or, instead, to feign refinement by having James drive them but with all three sisters crushed together? The decision was made by Elizabeth who insisted on driving the carriage so that James could be put to better use. "Why would I have him floundering about the grounds of Osborne Castle, chatting to maids, when he could be at home tending to the ivy on the side of the house?"

Once within the estate gates, Emma found much to admire. The trees lining the sweep on either side were magnificent and ancient. The building itself, while regal in its Tudor origins, was very recently and sympathetically added to with elegant wings on either side – displaying symmetry, taste and, with so many windows, an obvious desire for light and bright interiors. Even Lady Macbeth seemed impressed by the elegant, unfamiliar surroundings and moved briskly and confidently along the sweep to the front of the castle. When the ladies arrived at the door, they were informed that the Shaws, Penelope, Dr Harding and the Tomlinsons had already arrived. On entering, they perceived a grand entrance hall of marble floor and intricate plasterwork. Its size, Emma calculated, would comfortably accommodate all of Stanton's rooms. There was nothing to dislike within or without so far and they were directed to a room where the others, some dressed for riding, had already gathered and greeted them warmly.

A light breakfast was served and Emma regretted that she'd received only a quick, although cheery, acknowledgement from Mr Howard. The seating arrangements, which might have been orchestrated by design, did little to help for it saw Lord Osborne on one side of her and Tom Musgrave on the other, while Mr Howard was banished to the other end of the table between Penelope and Margaret. Elizabeth did not fare much better and could be heard muttering "Good Lord" as she took her seat between Mr Shaw and Solomon Tomlinson.

"If I did not know better, Miss Emma, I would believe you were avoiding us," started Tom Musgrave.

"I have been busy of late, sir."

"Indeed you have, Miss Watson," continued Tom Musgrave. "I was most disturbed to learn from Charles this week that you have been teaching him for several weeks, not a dozen yards from Osborne Castle and we knew nothing of it."

"I believe Lady Osborne knew – perhaps it did not matter a great deal. It is only some instruction in languages."

"It matters a *great* deal, Miss Watson."

"Tom, let it be," interrupted Lord Osborne. "What he means is that we should have liked to pay our respects while you were in the vicinity, to applaud your taking our young friend under your wing. Perhaps we may do so yet."

"Thank you," replied Emma, not knowing what else to say.

Meanwhile across the table, Solomon Tomlinson, giddy at sitting next to Miss Shaw, was attempting to address the entire table. He wished to impress Louisa with the solemnity of his convictions and have her observe how well he spoke when a group was gathered. Unfortunately, he chose a topic that was to offend several of those present.

"You read novels, Miss Shaw; I am surprised."

"That I read, sir, or at their being novels?" Louisa answered, amused.

"Reading is such a dreadful occupation but everyone is at it nowadays – their heads stuck in a book. It makes simpletons of the masses and would best be left to scholars and clergymen. What say you, Howard?"

Mr Howard said nothing, busied himself with his drink and coughed into his napkin.

Not to be put off, Solomon tried elsewhere. "And you Miss Emma, what say you? I must confess I was surprised when I heard that you have quite a fine library at Stanton, considering its size. What say you in defence of reading?"

"My father fits the two professions you described as best suited to the pursuit, for he is both a clergyman and a scholar, so perhaps that is why we possess so many. I feel the real reason, however, is the great enjoyment it gives him and he always encouraged his children to read. He quotes Shakespeare – *'ignorance is the curse of God; knowledge is the wing wherewith we fly to Heaven'*."

"Absolutely, absolutely," interjected Dr Harding.

"And where did it ever get Shakespeare? I can boast that I have never yet read Shakespeare and I have it from the most learned of my acquaintance in Oxford that he is going quite out of fashion. No one will know his name in twenty years or so. I, myself, have found that a handful of quality, comprehensive works on moral guidance is sufficient for the literary wants of ordinary people. Women, in particular, instead of reading, had best stick with their needlework and samplers and leave books to educated gentlemen."

Mr Shaw muttered beneath his breath, "Had I a needle to hand, at this moment, it is not into a sampler I would stick it."

"As you can see, I keep a pocket edition of *Fordyce's Sermons for Young Women* about me at all times. You would be surprised at how frequently I have to call upon its wisdom. The worst novels, of course, are written by women. Hannah More being the exception. Her *Practical Piety* and *The Character of St Paul* I have flicked through at the great library in Oxford and find her intentions were as they should be. Do you not agree?"

Mrs Blake coughed, Miss Osborne struggled to hide a snigger, Lady Osborne was flushed and uneasy, Lord Osborne looked bored and Miss Shaw stared at her plate.

Despite the lack of encouragement, Solomon continued in earnest, for his voice sounded particularly well to him this morning and in this large room it made a sort of echo. He could not back down now just when he was getting into his stride.

"A woman writer is an abominable thing. Only men were designed to succeed in the field ... women have never excelled at it and never will. Men display intellect, reason and wit. In women, it shows an ugly independence of spirit and a personal impurity, for how can she write of scandal and intrigue unless she has an intimate knowledge of same? Here, I have a page marked on this very subject which I will find you now."

Emma, just then, heard Lady Osborne, who sat on the other side of Tom Musgrave, whisper, "I beseech you, Tom, change the subject if possible. I am quite distressed."

"Mr Tomlinson, please spare us the sermon, I had rather wait for Sunday service," cried out Tom Musgrave.

"Mr Tomlinson," agreed Mr Shaw, "there now exists in the ambience a crack of about seven foot by eight. What say you speak of something more light of tone? If I had known that the objective of the morning was to bore, I would gladly tell you all of my forthcoming trip to Vienna, where I shall reside for a year or so. I must make a report on the zoo there, *Tiergarten Schönbrunn*, for the Linnean Society."

"I must continue. I am an instrument of God. It was He who chose, not I." Mr Tomlinson cleared his throat and proceeded to read aloud from his book:

"What shall we say of certain books, which we are assured (for we have not read them) are in their nature so shameful, in the tendency, so pestiferous and contain such rank treason against the royalty of Virtue, such horrible violation of all decorum, that she who can bear to peruse them must in her soul be a prostit ..."

"Enough!" Mr Howard interrupted. "One more word, Mr Tomlinson, and you will ne'er share a pulpit with me from this day forth."

Solomon Tomlinson snapped his book shut but tipped his chin further in the air. All was awkwardness and silence until Tom Musgrave broke in.

"This is nonsense talk, Mr Tomlinson. I know of lady writers and hold them in the highest regard and esteem. Come, let us talk of the hunt. Lord Osborne, tell me, is your horse mended?"

But Solomon was not to be silenced. "You all surprise me and I am ashamed that none agree with me. You know not what wicked works exist. What of this new lady novelist, Mrs Oliver? Where is her husband and why is he not forbidding her endeavours? I dare say it is another name for that romantic author Charlotte Smith, with her lusty tales of infidelity."

"I think not," Louisa interrupted. "Mrs Smith has been dead these ten years, at least, whereas Mrs Oliver published only last year. I have all her novels."

"I have read Mrs Oliver's works," said Mr Howard, to Emma's surprise, and a secret smile was exchanged between him and Lady Osborne. "I find them most wonderful. The latest novel of which you speak has a very smart clergyman in it."

"Really, well ...?"

"... and a very stupid clergyman also."

"There, you see, a tale of lies, for there is no such thing as a stupid clergyman. Each is sanctified on High to carry out the work of the Lord and bring His flock onto safer ground. One cannot be anointed and stupid."

Mr Shaw whispered across the table to Emma, "Indeed, one can. I have heard his sermon and can assure you that the only place he brings the Lord's flock is around in circles."

"I will write to the *London Gazette* tomorrow, denouncing the writings of this Mrs Oliver and her work of the devil. No self-respecting man will allow his wife or daughters to read such stuff when they have read the valid points that I make."

"I believe you will find," interrupted Elizabeth, "that no action is more likely to cause a panic for the purchase of her book than that which you recommend. Everyone wishes to read those books that are denounced. So if you wish to add greatly to her purse, then proceed, sir, with abandon."

"And I believe it very ungentlemanly behaviour to speak like this in Lady Osborne's home. Is this how generosity is to be rewarded – with a lecture on women? Very ungentlemanly, I must say," said Mr Shaw.

"Ungentlemanly and boring," Miss Tomlinson uttered aloud. "Do not tire the company with your rant on lady writers, brother. I tell you time and again, if men wrote books that were less boring, then women would read them. There are hardly three books at home that do not put me to sleep on opening them. It is why I choose to ride rather than read."

Lady Osborne took the hint. "Yes, and on that matter it is time we left the table and retired to the drawing-room. The horses will be brought around shortly." With her satin gown sweeping the marble floor, she moved hastily and led the party from the room.

Not quite finished, Mr Tomlinson continued to no one in particular, "There is one woman, whom I have already mentioned – an evangelical lady of the highest intelligence and of whom I would not be ashamed to associate myself – Mrs Hannah More, the famous authoress. Now here we have a woman who can write. Here we have intelligence and zealousness ... and what does she advise of ladies – the only words from her book which I learned by heart, was that women should develop *a submissive temper and a forbearing spirit*. Hear, hear, I say!" But nobody listened and Mr Tomlinson, deprived of his audience, sniffed the air and followed them with an unaffected appearance of triumph for, in his head, his argument had carried the day.

The drawing-room was large with comfortable seating, elegant décor and magnificent views from the window. Emma hoped, as she sat by Elizabeth, that Mr Howard would finally join her. At first, he and Mr Shaw stood together laughing and conversing as though they were old friends and just when he smiled at her and began to move in her direction, he was called by the other men around the mantelpiece for his opinion on some matter. Elizabeth looked across the room at the men who stood admiring or criticising Lord Osborne's new riding boots and said, "Look at them, sister." Emma dutifully turned to observe Tom Musgrave, Dr Harding, Solomon Tomlinson, Mr Howard, Mr Shaw and, of course, Lord Osborne in animated conversation.

"It is true that God and their mothers must indeed love them but really, Emma, there isn't a perfect one among them. In fact, if the good Lord would stir them up in a large pot, He might have one right man made. Do not look at me like that. Even with all your goodness, you know that I speak the truth. Do I, or do I not, speak the truth? Out with it, out! The only thing that one should 'keep in' is good spirits."

"Mr Howard is without fault," whispered Emma, eyes lowered.

"Oh, do take care, Emma, if you are considering taking a faultless man as your husband! A perfect spouse would be a terrible affliction. If a wife cannot point out all those areas where her husband needs improvement, I fear they may have very little else to discuss."

Louisa came to join them and complained of a headache. Elizabeth, blaming her proximity to Solomon Tomlinson at breakfast and his ceaseless ranting as the cause of the ailment, recommended fresh air as the best cure and offered to walk with her in the shrubbery. Louisa agreed and both women, wishing to leave as quietly as possible, informed Lady Osborne in a whisper and excused themselves.

Emma was considering joining Mrs Blake when the

group of men suddenly broke up and moved about – Margaret, who sat like a Babylonian princess, called Tom Musgrave to ask his opinion on a new shawl, Dr Harding complimented Lady Osborne on the fine view from the window, Mr Shaw made enquiries as to the whereabouts of his sister and just as it appeared that Mr Howard was once more moving in her direction, Lord Osborne called out to Emma, "Come, Miss Watson, come at once. I must show you my fine display of rifles. They are in a glass cabinet in the big hall."

"Oh, no, sir, I thank you. Such things are of little interest to me."

"But as we danced, at the ball, you asked me most particularly about hunting, my dogs and rifles. There is not a similar display to be had in the county. Miss Tomlinson declares she would wager that Lord Nelson has not so fine a collection. Come now. I must insist. Come this way, Miss Emma, if you please."

Lord Osborne looked over his shoulder to where Tom Musgrave stood, who, taking the hint, added, "Miss Watson, please humour his lordship with your presence. If you do not, I fear he may drag me along and I have seen them at least ten thousand times before."

Emma coloured with both embarrassment and anger. Lord Osborne's persistence and now Tom Musgrave's cajoling made any sense of obligation she had felt vanish. She wished she had not come. As it was now obvious that they would not relent and any continuation in this manner would soon draw the attention of all others upon them, she acquiesced.

Had Elizabeth been present, Emma would have insisted on her accompanying them. In her absence, she would have to ensure that they return to the room as quickly as possible, so that no mischief might be construed by the others.

Lord Osborne was an eccentric, to be sure, and when she had learned of the cruelty that he had endured as a child, she had felt compassion, but now her sympathy was decreasing with her every step away from the drawing-room. Lord Osborne led her down the hallway, walking swiftly to the great hall. It was a greater distance than she had imagined, necessitating their walking down several corridors and one flight of stairs. Only now did Emma understand the magnitude of the castle and what a cost it must have been to modernise it with such excellent taste.

When they reached the rifle cabinet, Emma stood dutifully looking into the case while Lord Osborne started a lengthy monologue on all the types, their age and use. Finally, he noted in a disappointed tone, "You do not seem moved by these wonderful specimens, Miss Watson. I fear I bore you."

Emma felt that it might have been a good thing after all that Elizabeth was not present for she surely would have answered, "Why, yes, Lord Osborne, you do."

Instead Emma reached for the most honest and polite response she could find that would enable their retreat back to the others.

"It is true that I do not have a particular interest in weapons, sir, but the paintings I saw on the gallery to get here were quite magnificent. And if you do not mind, sir, we are gone quite a while and I should like to return to my friends."

"Of course, we shall return at once. I do hope you will

discover in time much more to like at the castle, Miss Watson."

Emma walked on, not wishing to interpret his meaning, and therefore changed the subject to one that showed interest: "Your mother has, I believe, made great changes here and in the garden. It is to her credit, I am sure."

"Yes, it was a dark place when I was a child. Lots of the rooms were unused and windows boarded shut. Humphry Repton has been engaged to design a terrace at the front; the walled garden was a jungle of sorts but my mother has made it a very pleasant place for ladies to walk and sit."

Sensing the conversation again hinting at her becoming intimate with the inhabitants of the castle, Emma once again changed the topic. "She is thought of highly at the parsonage, where I believe she has displayed a most benevolent and interested patronage."

"Yes, Mr Howard can do no wrong in her eyes, nor she in his. Ah we are back, now, may I fetch you fresh coffee?"

"No, I thank you."

On returning to the room, Emma sought out the reassurance of Mr Howard's countenance at once. Finding him, across the room, she smiled but it was not returned. He looked away, turned his back to Emma, and continued speaking to Lady Osborne. Turning again suddenly, he called out to the room, "Come now, I am anxious for air. The horses must be ready these fifteen minutes, at least. Let us be gone. Come, Miss Tomlinson, help me move these idlers."

Confused and hurt, Emma watched as he strode from the room, waiting for one last look to prove she had nothing to worry about, but, for her troubles, she received only an unmistakeable stare in her direction as he left – of hurt, betrayal and anger. Miss Tomlinson followed him, loudly ordering all the riders to be up and away, wishing all others a good day and a safe trip home. The remaining riders left in sequence, Lord Osborne being the last, wishing Emma a good day and repeating his hopes to call upon her when she was teaching Charles.

As she sat back in her chair in disbelief, Emma nodded distractedly as Mrs Blake spoke to her, not aware to what she was agreeing. She could think only of Mr Howard. Something must be the matter for such an unmistakeable change to occur. The difference between his present air and that of earlier this morning was great. What could she have done to deserve such a look? Surely Mr Howard had not believed that she had encouraged Lord Osborne's attentions or that she had wished to be alone with him. How could he draw such a conclusion, he who she felt knew her so well?

Louisa returned to the room in better spirits than when she had left and Elizabeth found herself approached by Mr Shaw who thanked her for her kindness. That a man who never offered praise was genuine in his gratitude confused Elizabeth who was ever on the defence in his company. She answered that it was no trouble, that Louisa was a sweet girl and how strange it was that they were brother and sister. It sounded more dismissive than she had intended and Mr Shaw retreated quickly. For a moment she regretted that the opportunity for goodwill to develop between them was lost, but consoled herself that his good opinion was not worth pursuing.

The rest of the party broke up shortly afterwards and as Emma took her leave of Penelope, her sharp and observant sister commented, "My, but your Mr Howard is very out of sorts today. I am not convinced that he is at all amiable. That is the way with these young men in love – a problem, I confess, that I never encountered with the dear doctor. His flighty days were long behind him before we met."

With a heart confused and heavy, Emma returned home to Stanton with her sisters and excused herself for an hour to lie down. She retired to her bedroom where she was free to punish herself all afternoon for the imagined offences with which she must have injured Mr Howard.

That evening, when they found themselves alone, Elizabeth noticed that Emma had not touched her food.

"Emma, I do declare, you eat nothing. You are either deeply in love or heartbroken. Which is it today?"

A comment so close to the truth caught Emma off guard and soon she was unable to quell the tears that now wished to flow. Elizabeth sat next to her and held her close.

"There now, I am so sorry. I had guessed when you returned from the castle so downcast, that all was not well. Did Lord Osborne say something to offend you when you were alone?"

Shaking her head, Emma told Elizabeth all about her feelings for Mr Howard and her confusion over his reaction when she returned to the room.

"I dare say he was jealous, which is a good thing, for if he is to propose he will do so now in a hurry, for fear Lord Osborne gets there first. Emma, you have two men to choose from. I, for my part, should settle for half a man at this point."

"Do you really believe it will encourage him to propose? I had not thought of that. His look was so unforgiving – it was like a knife cut through me. I shall never forget it."

"Of course I believe he will propose! Although I hardly feel he deserves you now, if this be the way he acts at the first misunderstanding. How dare he act so? And I was just beginning to like him a great deal. I hope it is not a sign of a temperamental man. If it is, you had best go with Lord Osborne. At least you will always know where you stand with him and you can throw cabbages at the parsonage from one of your turrets."

Emma gave a watery smile but soon turned to sobbing again.

Elizabeth apologised. "Oh, I am sorry, I did not intend to make fun. It is just that either man is a desirable match in my eyes. My advice to you is as follows – give Mr Howard an opportunity to redeem himself but if he proves to be inconsistent in his feelings, you may still have Lord Osborne. That is all I say."

It was futile attempting to convince the eternally cheerful Elizabeth that Emma did not desire a choice. She wished for the man she loved to love her back and, if he were willing to take a penniless bride, to go through life by his side. Although soothed somewhat by Elizabeth, a couple of sleepless nights were assured, for Emma was due at Wickstead on Thursday morning. She would know then by Mr Howard's behaviour whether, or not, he was lost to her forever.

CHAPTER FOURTEEN

Thursday did indeed satisfy Emma's curiosity. Mr Howard was not available to meet with her at any point and Mrs Blake, upset and embarrassed, made his excuses instead.

"My dear Emma," she whispered, "my brother has been in his study all morning. There is so much to do in the parish at present ... He is very busy, quite overtaken with work ... I will send Charles with you as far as the stile."

"There is no need," Emma forced a smile. "I am quite content to make my way home as I make my way hither. Thank you most kindly for the offer."

Looking from the classroom window a little later, however, Emma noticed Mr Howard crossing the lawn. He stopped to look up in her direction and instead of returning to the house, as it appeared he was meaning to do, turned suddenly into the garden. When it was time to leave, Emma took her shawl and crept past his study to the door and let herself out. She walked slowly down the sweep and through the gates, hoping that at any moment she would hear him call out her name – that he had finished his work, that he was walking her home, that her fears were unfounded. All was silence but for birdsong. She walked on, immersed in a sadness that she did not know how to shake. He despised her, of this she was now convinced, and there was nothing she could do to clear her name or un-taint herself in his eyes. How could she be nothing to him, when no two souls had been as close?

Elizabeth met Emma with a cheerful yet questioning look, to which she shook her head. She allowed herself to be enfolded and comforted and as they parted said, "Please sister, my heart aches. Let us speak no more of this."

The following morning, Mrs Ellingham left in the height of good spirits, having developed a deep fondness for Mr Watson and his girls. She had been useful where she was needed and appreciated, which gave her an excessive sense of satisfaction while also filling a large gap created in her life by the lengthy absence of her seafaring son. Even Mr Watson allowed that he would miss her kindly face about the place.

Emma attempted to banish her own sunken spirits by insisting on taking their guest to the inn at Dorking where she would then catch the early post-chaise home.

"Harold will be glad to see you," she commented to Mrs Ellingham.

"I believe he will, for he gets no pound cake like his mother's, no matter where he travels, or at least that is what he tells his mother."

"Parting with you is not easy, but knowing that a hungry young sailor will benefit from your wonderful cake makes it a little easier."

"You girls made me so very much at home and even

your father was kind and attentive when his health permitted it. Your mother would be so proud of how you all turned out. She was such fun to be around. How she loved to laugh and often did so until the tears ran down her face, bless her soul. I grew up in a house of men and had only my husband and son at home for many years, it has been such a treat for me to be among so many dear women. Would that I lived closer."

"You are welcome to visit Stanton at any time – and Harold. We would love to have you come to stay. Yes, my mother loved to laugh, but you too, Mrs Ellingham; you are forever in good humour."

"Well then, I must tell you my secret. It is that I wish everyone well. It is quite a joyful habit, I can tell you, and the more disgruntled the recipient, the more well I wish them. It can make them quite angry at first but eventually they soften for I just keep at it."

Old Lady Macbeth trotted heavily on and the ladies, comfortable in each other's company, rode much of the way in silence, only talking now and again to point out walkers ascending Box Hill or note an unusual feature of the landscape. Finally, they arrived at the White Hart and Emma, wishing to avail of this opportunity to say "good day" to Penelope and her friends, saw Mrs Ellingham to her coach before entering the inn to find Penelope, her husband and the Shaws within, all just finished breakfast and delighted with the surprise of seeing her there.

"So Mrs Ellingham has left. I do hope she returns again soon so that you girls can get out. It is such a bore to have no sisters married, all my friends are shocked when I tell them."

"The conversation turns to marriage yet again," said Mr

Shaw. "I wish I could ban the subject. Ovid, you know, was exiled from Rome for writing *The Art of Love*. The sensible Romans got so wearied of listening to his incessant talk that they threw him out of town. It is a practice I would re-introduce if I could."

"You make fun of us all, brother. Everyone except you wishes for marriage and a happy one at that. Surely you do not wish to grow old without a companion?"

"I do not fear growing old alone, my dear. I have my studies and cynicism to keep me company. Women, however, are obsessed with the happy ending that they believe the matrimonial state will bring. They have not the patience to stick with the married couple for long enough to examine the consequences some years later but instead have quickly and conveniently moved on to the next silly couple who must be married off."

The innkeeper entered just then to clear away the plates and Emma's attention was drawn by Penelope who wished to know if her bonnet could be made less ugly, when noisy yet confident footsteps approached the room. A moment later, the door opened to admit Solomon Tomlinson.

"Good morning to you all. What a fortunate coincidence. I had heard you leave tomorrow and I feared I would not see you before you departed."

The surprised group remained silent but smiled politely, excepting Mr Shaw who scowled openly and the innkeeper who hurriedly departed. There was silence for a few moments. Solomon kept his stare fixed on an increasingly red-faced Miss Shaw, which he took as a compliment to himself.

"As it so happens, I intend to visit Chichester on business shortly. There is a preacher there whose works have impressed me greatly. He is a Mr Edmunds. You have heard of him perhaps, Miss Shaw?"

"No, we have not heard of him, thank you, Mr Tomlinson," interrupted Mr Shaw. "We are not followers of the hot molten coals and fire school of Christianity which you seem to prefer."

"You would do well to re-read The Book of Revelation, Mr Shaw, to learn what God's plans are for Satan and the ungodly who are cast, we are told, into a lake burning with brimstone."

"Indeed, quite! Well I feel we must retire and commence packing. It may take some time. Come, sister."

"I should like to call on you when I am in Chichester. I have not finalised my lodgings as yet but I will leave my card if I find no one at home."

"Absolutely, absolutely," said Dr Harding, for which he received a pinch from his wife for his interference.

"I have a feeling I will be from home a great deal but by all means leave your card. Good day, sir." Mr and Miss Shaw retreated from the deeply bowing clergyman. Then Mr Tomlinson scanned the room, contemplating who, next in importance, was worthy of his condescension. He settled on the doctor and after receiving a number of short sentences comprising of "Absolutelys", "Indeeds" and "Capitals" he left the company.

"Of course you can have Lord Osborne, Emma, but it may be a good idea to put yourself around at Chichester too," said Penelope. "Through our friendship with Lady

Edgeworth, we know many wealthy and titled gentlemen. Unfortunately, they are rarely both at once."

"Absolutely true, my dear," added Dr Harding.

"I must insist," continued Penelope, "that either you or Elizabeth come away with us tomorrow, to spend Christmas at Chichester. I asked Margaret first but she refuses to leave Tom Musgrave for so long when things appear promising in that quarter. Ha! I laughed in her face when she said it. But you and Elizabeth – it is quite a pitiful state of affairs. As the only married woman in the family, I must lead the rest of you on this matter. Father may live for goodness knows how long and you will both be old maids. Don't look at me like that, Emma. You none of you see Father as I do. He is playing up on his complaints. Even old Dr Richards is blind to it."

"Such a picture you paint, Penelope." Emma did not know whether to laugh or take insult.

"And my dear husband already supports a widowed sister in Coventry and her girls – far too generously. I dare say they thought he would remain single forever and were greatly disappointed that he did not. Nobody wants a rich uncle to wed. So you see, we can do no more for you than to see you well married."

"I'm sure my dear, if it came to it, we –" attempted Dr Harding but Penelope was not to be interrupted.

"I did mention it to Elizabeth last night but let you decide between yourselves. It matters little to me, whether it is one or the other of you. The case is more urgent, perhaps, for Elizabeth, but a penniless former heiress is not easy to shift either. I shall give all my energy to one of you first and then move onto the other. What say you, my dear doctor, to us finding husbands for my sisters?"

As she made her solitary journey home, Emma contemplated the offer that Penelope had made and the more she thought of it, the more she approved of it. Such a scheme would enable her to escape, with ease and discretion, the awkward situation she found herself in. It was a way to avoid pain at Wickstead and to distance herself from Lord Osborne – that his enthusiasm might wane in her absence. What could be more natural than visiting her sister's new home in Chichester – a sister whom she had not met for fourteen years. They had much to talk of and so many of her sister's friends to meet. She would become more acquainted with the doctor and his family. It was a wonderful scheme.

As Lady Macbeth drearily turned in through the gates at Stanton, Emma found herself wishing that, for this current offer to visit Chichester, Elizabeth would show little interest. Indulging in thoughts of an escape, she imagined herself removed from her troubles. Packing for the visit would take little time and she could take only one, perhaps two, good dresses with her. Nanny would send for James who could drive her to the inn early the following morning and by this time tomorrow the distance between her and her sorrows would be great.

When she spoke to Elizabeth, however, and saw how her eyes danced at the prospect of balls, suitors and a change of scene, she swallowed her disappointment and kindly encouraged her to go instead. Likewise, Elizabeth reluctantly objected.

"But I cannot leave you here alone for Christmas, with only Margaret. You will have to do everything for Father for you know she is quite useless."

"I insist," replied Emma. "Father is more mobile and much improved of late and besides, I wish to finish at Wickstead and this will give me the excuse I need. The tutoring had always been of a temporary nature – only to last while there was additional help at home. I confess, for reasons which you alone know, it would be a great relief to get out of the obligation. Tomorrow shall be my final day of tutoring young Charles."

"Oh Emma, I am sorry. Are you absolutely certain?"

"Yes, I am. Besides, I long to learn how you will manage such a journey in the close confinement of a carriage with Mr Shaw."

"I have no doubt as to Mr Shaw's fate. I shall murder him within the first five miles and, when the others sleep, I will kick him out of the carriage. I promise to write to you, Emma, and more often than before."

With mixed feelings, Emma left for Wickstead on the day of Elizabeth's departure. She must inform them that she could no longer come to teach, severing the connection with those people among whom she had been happiest. She spoke to Mrs Blake and Charles on her arrival and informed them of her news. Mrs Blake's kindness and her assurance of the gratitude of herself and her brother, who was away from home just then, almost brought Emma to tears. Only the internal whispering of "Mr Howard does not care for me" prevented it. Charles looked forlorn but was consoled by Mrs Blake's promise that it would mean more time at the stables. A weak assurance was given by Emma of calling again someday or other, if her father's health permitted her absence from home.

That day's lesson with Charles went ahead as normal, until interrupted by a loud rap at the front door. Charles, running to the window, shouted, "It is Lord Osborne and Miss Osborne." A visit from Lord Osborne was unwelcome, on this of all days, but Emma consoled herself that at least it could never happen again. The door to the classroom was opened some minutes later by Mrs Blake. The look of surprise on her face indicated that she was not used to such honoured guests calling to check on the education of her children. Charles delighted in telling the visitors some of the many words and phrases he had learned. Miss Osborne, who must have been made come by her brother, appeared amused, complimented Emma on her skill and noted that it was a strange occupation for a lady to choose to undertake. Meanwhile, Lord Osborne went to the window and said something of always having hated learning.

When a silence fell, Mrs Blake explained. "How fortunate it is that you came today, as it is Miss Watson's final day with us. The household at Stanton has been reduced from four ladies to two so she must care for her father. We will miss her greatly."

"This is extremely inconvenient," said Lord Osborne, turning around suddenly. "I had not expected it. Why can you not find a woman in the village to tend to your father? Charles had best continue his studies. You had best teach him."

Surprised and annoyed that she was required to defend

herself, Emma responded, "For some, the preference is to spend time with their parent when they are unwell. I have shirked my responsibility for fourteen years and would like to be with my father now."

"But I had hoped you would call on my mother after lessons some day and learn of her plans for the terrace. This cannot happen now."

"I fear not."

With a "Very well, good day," Lord Osborne swiftly left the room, followed by his sister and Mrs Blake scurrying behind.

It was some minutes before Emma could return to any semblance of calm but she soon found thoughts to console. Firstly, that Lord Osborne could not visit her again so conveniently as he had just done and secondly that he seemed annoyed with her on leaving. This could only aid her attempts at quelling his affections. Mr Howard, of course, would hear of Lord Osborne's visit. Would he think she had encouraged it? Might he be angry or indifferent to learn of it? The contemplation of his reaction, the necessity of finishing at Wickstead in addition to the unwelcome visit that afternoon, ensured that Emma remained irritable for the rest of the lesson, though she hid it well from Charles. It was with gratitude, therefore, that she placed one foot before the other on her walk home, wishing the distance between herself and Wickstead to be even greater.

Emma kept herself busy in the days that followed, taking on the extra tasks brought about by the absence of Mrs Ellingham and Elizabeth. These duties had unexpectedly increased, for by the end of the first week, Mr Watson, whose spirits had sunk and whose bones ailed him, was fully bedridden again. When Emma secured occasional periods of respite from her father's care, she indulged in lonely walks where nature could provide the balm for a heart that felt it would never heal and comfort for a tired body and mind that did not sleep. At night she prayed for her family but most especially that God would restore her father's health and deliver to Elizabeth that happiness in life which she deserved. She asked Him to lessen her own pain and to ensure that the coming month would be a quiet one, without sightings or mention of Messrs Howard, Musgrave, Tomlinson or Lord Osborne. But she knew in her heart that even the Almighty could not deliver on this last request, for despite Emma's avoidance of company and balls, there was no quenching Margaret's love of gossip.

CHAPTER FIFTEEN

Time moved on, as time is wont to do and, as Christmas approached, Emma found that although she was still not her old self, she did have strength to get up and get on with her day. Her heart was broken and her beloved sister absent but she had found ways that, while they did not make her happy, prevented further pain by distracting her a great deal. Preparations for Christmas were necessary and there were gifts to be distributed to the poor in the village. Her father's health had not improved since he had returned to his bed, which also preoccupied her as she had to tend to him often and worry over him a great deal.

Margaret was easier to contend with than she had anticipated. Emma's volunteering to stay at home with their father meant more balls for her and this, together with allowing her to prattle away without being obliged to listen to a response, kept Margaret in the best of form. She loved gossip in every form – the creation, spreading, dissecting and discussing of it. Fortunately for her, she was one of a group of like-minded friends who never tired of feeding their mutual need for "news" – tirelessly and, in their own minds, generously going out of their way to do so. Margaret usually returned from balls in a frenzy, with news that was of little interest to Emma. Occasionally she teased with "your Mr Howard this" or "your Lord Osborne that" but it was only in the most trivial of matters such as what they wore or what Tom Musgrave said to them. One piece of news of Margaret's, however, did catch Emma's attention.

"It is all 'Miss Osborne this and Miss Osborne that' with Captain Hunter these days. He no longer favours Miss Edwards."

"Really? Can it be so?" Emma asked, closing her book and sitting forward in her chair.

"Yes, quite. Mrs Edwards was furious that Mary – who understood from his friends that the Captain was to approach her for the first dance, but instead stepped out with Miss Osborne – was shunned the entire evening. She insisted that we leave early despite her husband winning at cards. It quite enraged me as I was just then speaking with Tom Musgrave."

"He did not dance once with Mary?"

"Not once, but he danced several times with Miss Osborne. It was said that she has been encouraging him for some time. My loyalty is torn. Of course, I feel dreadful for Miss Edwards and annoyed that it forced our early departure, but I must also consider Tom Musgrave's connection with the Osbornes. Miss Osborne and I may become intimates someday."

Emma pitied her friend. Though she was not particularly fond of the Captain, she knew that Mary was and now, no doubt, was nursing a sore heart. It was a feeling she was all too familiar with and one which she wished Miss Edwards had been spared.

Within a few days of this news, Emma received a visit from Mrs Edwards and her daughter, who made enquiries into Mr Watson's health and then turned to the topic which was foremost on all their minds.

"My dear girl, I apologise that we have not visited you until now but we had other matters to contend with," said Mrs Edwards, eyeing her daughter who was somewhat pale and had her eyes lowered. "We have not had the pleasure of your company at any assembly of late and would have called sooner but for all the Christmas comings and goings. If the good Lord had any mercy on us, he would have been born in June, for it is quite shocking to be obliged to leave one's fireplace in the winter."

"Please do not apologise, Mrs Edwards, you are welcome here anytime. I hope all is well with you."

"Very well, I thank you. But let us not stand on ceremony, for we are friends and may speak freely. You have no doubt heard of the fickle nature of Captain Hunter."

"I heard a little." Emma looked sympathetically at Miss Edwards.

"Nonsense! You are the sister of Miss Margaret Watson, the Town-Crier, are you not?"

"Yes, ma'am." Emma tried not to smile.

"Well then, you know as much as we do, and, most likely, more. I did not like the man, I confess, and did not wish him for our daughter; however, his ungentlemanly and public humiliation of Mary is quite appalling."

"Please, Mamma. It was not sudden. I had suspected a change."

"Regardless. It was despicable. All I say is God help England, if this is the character of person who is to defend us against Mr Bonaparte. We are surely doomed. He will be the first to run for the hills."

"Mamma, please. You promised we should stop talking on this subject. Miss Watson, please tell me, have you heard from Elizabeth since she left?"

"Only that she has arrived safely and seems delighted already."

"I am glad to hear it," said Mrs Edwards, momentarily becoming less irritated. "I have no doubt that meeting many new people will be a good thing for Elizabeth. She has a social heart, dear girl."

"Yes; however, she will also likely see some familiar faces. The Shaws, as you know, live nearby and also, Mr Solomon Tomlinson has promised to visit as he will be in Chichester later this week."

"Indeed!" responded Mrs Edwards. "If that is the case then I believe he made it his business to be in Chichester later this week. We all witnessed his attempt to attach himself to that sweet young Miss Shaw at the last ball she attended and, unfortunately, he does not give up easily."

"I believe she is quite safe."

"Quite safe, you are sure?"

"Yes, indeed."

"Good, very good. There has been a great deal of wastage in that man's life – the parable about the talents springs to mind. When I think of all the smart young people deprived of an education while one was thrown away on him, I get quite furious. You are aware that he was not always destined for the church?"

"I did hear that he was not suited to his father's business in banking and, therefore, studied for the church."

"Well, there are few that know this fact and I tell you now in confidence so please do not tell a soul, especially your sister Margaret. Solomon Tomlinson did work at his father's bank for a short while and in that time lost the great sum of £30,000, which was not his to lose."

"I am shocked. Such a sum. A fortune. How could it have happened? Was he tricked in some way?"

"It was he who was performing the trick – an act of disappearance. In some moment of foolishness, perhaps an attempt to win the admiration of all, he accessed money and invested how and where he pleased. He did not seek the permission of, or consult with, any other person – his father or the clients whose money he misappropriated. He was imprudent and vain and when he lost everything and his scandalous behaviour became known to his family, he bore no responsibility. The miracle was how his parents succeeded in keeping the law out of the affair and ensuring that the entire episode remained secret. His father lost almost everything he had in covering the losses and some of his clients took their investments elsewhere. We, as one of the casualties, were repaid and as we are old friends of the Tomlinsons we remained with them, once we were reassured that their son would never again work with his father. I am afraid I have shocked you, Emma, your eyes could not grow any wider."

"Yes, I am surprised. He advocates so strongly for eternal damnation and the unforgiveness of sins yet he himself has been shown such compassion and mercy. I am shocked more than I can say and cannot reconcile the two versions."

"Between Solomon Tomlinson, Captain Hunter and the slippery Tom Musgrave, I am quite sick of young men. They are not all as steady as your brother Samuel, Miss Watson, who I must say looks remarkably like you around the eyes in this light. Perhaps, if I drop my objection to the opposite sex, you may let him know that he is quite welcome to call on us the next time he plans to stay at Stanton. My husband was just saying how he feels he might fill in for your father on occasion at their Whist Club. He said he had never witnessed a fairer player than your Sam."

Emma nodded her agreement and, delighted for her brother, noted how the colour returning to Miss Edwards' cheeks became her so well.

Another week of sitting with her father and ignoring the gossip of her sister went by and another of Elizabeth's letters arrived, apologising for the delay and promising to be more reliable in future. She acknowledged receipt of Emma's letter and though it was played down, stated her concern for their father's deterioration, hoping it was nothing to worry about but ordering Emma to write immediately if it was. She then turned to another subject.

... and you never reminded me to satisfy your curiosity with regards to our journey here and whether I killed Mr Shaw in the first ten miles or merely beat him and tied him to the back of the carriage, that the dogs

might chase him. You will be shocked to hear that I did neither! As we left the White Hart, Mr Shaw and his sister sat on one side of the carriage while I sat next to Dr Harding and Penelope. As you know, I admire Dr Harding exceedingly but he is not the smallest of men and I found myself quite crushed for the first fifteen miles, at which point we made our first stop. As I was the extra passenger, it was only right that it should be me being inconvenienced, but when we returned to the carriage, Mr Shaw spoke to me and asked that he sit next to Dr Harding for he had business he wished to discuss with him. I am afraid he insisted and, therefore, I sat very comfortably next to Louisa for the remainder of our trip while poor Mr Shaw could hardly breathe. Occasionally, I coaxed Penelope to join us on our side and Mr Shaw nodded his gratitude and availed of the opportunity to take a few additional deep breaths. Perhaps he is not the black-hearted villain that I had originally thought.

She then proceeded to describe what fun she was having in Chichester and how she was in receipt of the attentions of three eligible gentlemen.

… I dare not return home before I have captured one of them so, if Father be well enough, I may remain on for another fortnight. Penelope leaves for Bath then and I shall be happy to be back in Stanton with the promise of a ring on my finger. And it must be a long engagement for I will not abandon you to care for our father on your own, so whichever man I choose, he

must submit to that ...

Emma smiled at Elizabeth's positive expectations and willingness to fall in love at a moment's notice.

Later that afternoon, as Emma returned from a short walk in the copse, she spied a gentleman making his way towards her. At first, she thought it was Robert, then Mr Howard, and at last, as he was almost upon her, she correctly guessed it to be her brother Sam.

"At last, sister, we meet again," he said as he swung her around. "You are as light as a feather."

"Sam! How happy I am that you are here."

They had not met in years and rarely corresponded but Emma had retained a fondness for Sam that she had not borne for the others. It was a maternal, doting feeling – one often reserved for the youngest boy in a large family.

"I am so pleased to see you." Emma almost choked on the words. "You have come to see me at last. Come, let us go home, have tea and you can tell me all your news. Are you staying with us for Christmas? It would cheer us greatly, if you did."

"I cannot stay but a few minutes on this occasion, I am afraid. I was passing nearby and thought to call on you and Father, but next month, I have been assured, I can stay for a week."

Emma hid her disappointment.

"If that be so, let us talk as we walk."

"Yes, a great idea, a capital idea! Oh, Emma, how you've grown. We were both but children when last we met and dear mother, how long it is since she left us."

"I wish I had known her more. I envy you that."

"It must have been difficult for you but our aunt and uncle were kind, were they not? There were times, I confess, when I envied you at Claperton Park. It is a pity how it ended. We must hope that your fortune may swing back again and all will be well. Pray tell me, what is this I hear of you and Lord Osborne?"

"I do not know what you heard but there is nothing to it, I can assure you!"

"But I was informed that he is seeking your good opinion and that an engagement is imminent. Do not be shy, Emma, though your modesty does you credit. I have come to congratulate you, that is all. There need be no secrets between brother and sister."

He pressed her hand with warmth. Emma pulled it back.

"Sam, I tell you there is no understanding, nor have I any intention of encouraging it. It is some time since I met Lord Osborne and, I believe, I am quite out of favour with him. So you see, you have been misinformed."

Sam rubbed his forehead. "I apologise, Emma, it is just that I heard this news only yesterday from Dr Richards who happened to be in Guildford. He was all alarm that I knew nothing of it for he attends the castle regularly and assures me it is certain. You are spoken about daily at the castle. It is quite settled."

"Dear God, please do not say so."

"But Emma, if I may speak the truth, why would you not encourage it? He is a good man and holds you in the highest esteem. What wealth you will have – a title and a castle. You shall return to living as formerly, quite the lady of fashion. And think how this will benefit your family."

"Sam, please."

"What obstacle can there be? You are no longer an heiress jaunting about with your aunt in a low phaeton. It is Lord Osborne who condescends in this match, you must allow him that. What other impediment is there?"

"I wish to marry for love and ..." She said no more, wishing to mention neither her affections for Mr Howard nor her dislike of Lord Osborne.

"I understand," answered Sam. "I too wish to marry for love but Miss Edwards is too high for me so I cannot. My only hope is to advance as quickly as I can in my career. Yet if all my family were to marry well – that would also greatly increase my chances. Robert and Penelope have done exceedingly well. Elizabeth, I dare say, is doing her best in Chichester. You must be practical, Emma."

"Sam, you distress me with such talk. Please, we are here back at home. You visit Father and I will wait for you in the front room."

Emma remained in the parlour as Sam hurried upstairs, returning to his sister some ten minutes later.

"Father is not well, Emma, you must own that. I say it both as a son and as a medical man. There is no fighting spirit in him – one winter illness could take him. We must prepare for what the future holds and you may never get such an offer as Lord Osborne's again."

"Sam, let us speak no more on the subject and depart as friends. Let us wish each other happiness in marriage. I wish it for you and am charged with a commission of sorts, that may speed its progress. It is that you are held in higher regard by the Edwardses than formerly."

"How so, Emma?"

"Captain Hunter has withdrawn his attentions. The Edwardses called recently and even issued an invitation for you to visit when you next come to stay. Mr Edwards wishes you to play cards with him."

"Is it really so? How come you did you not say so before?"

"You did not give me the opportunity, so intent as you were to advise on matters of *my* heart. Your purpose in visiting was to persuade me to increase your prospects of a happy marriage while disregarding mine."

"Do not be so dramatic, Emma! You could perform in a play with such theatricals. I was merely encouraging you to take Osborne, for your own sake. Whether it be Osborne or another rich man, what is it to me? Oh, but I am pleased about the Edwardses. Do you really think I have a chance? Why, I must do. I will come to stay as soon as possible. Perhaps I will be granted leave in the next fortnight or so. This is quite wonderful. Goodbye, dear Emma."

Sam gave Emma a quick peck on the forehead and rushed from the room.

Nanny walked in to return the silverware she had been shining.

"Master Sam looked ever so concerned earlier, miss, and overcome with delight on leaving. Such a change of countenance."

"Yes, Nanny, and he has left me quite the opposite – delighted on meeting him and with a headache on his departure."

"Such are the young men today – bounding about and

stirring trouble where e'er they go. I will take the master up his dinner soon. You look ill, Miss Emma."

"Nanny, you are so good. I will call into him later. It is just a headache."

Nanny left for the kitchen. Emma had started idly tidying the bookshelves when a sudden and loud noise at the front of the house drew her attention to the window where an express pulled up. Another few moments and the driver was inside the hall, handing a letter to Emma. The writing signalled it was from Robert.

Emma, dear sister, I have, this morning, been approached by the most worthy of gentlemen, who sought my consent (in lieu of father's ill health) for your hand in marriage. I need not tell you his name, for you surely know of whom I refer. We were unaware of his being in town for some time already and though I pressed him to join us for dinner he declined for he wishes to return at once to Surrey. I have most heartily approved and come now myself to Stanton, surely to arrive by mid-morning tomorrow, by which time I hope to be making my congratulations. Your affectionate brother, Robert.

CHAPTER SIXTEEN

"Oh what to do?" exclaimed Emma. "This is too, too much." For a moment, she wondered if it was Mr Howard who had sought Robert out. It could not be, she decided, for he would have spoken directly to her and not sought permission from her brother first. It must have been Lord Osborne who had sought her brother's consent and by tomorrow morning Robert would be at Stanton, offering his congratulations. This meant that Lord Osborne must be on his way. Emma knew that she must act immediately, but how difficult it was to do so when there was an invalid parent to care for and her sister was away with friends. She would write an express to Elizabeth, insisting she return at once and allow Emma to go in her stead. She must send James out to fetch Margaret. Oh, she should have taken Penelope up on her offer to go to Chichester. Perhaps then this would have been avoided.

She went to the desk, grabbed paper and ink and with shaking hand began her letter. A familiar sound, however, indicated that it was too late. The unmistakeable rap of Lord Osborne's riding crop could be heard at the door. She ran to the parlour door to tell Nanny not to let him in but it was too late, he was in the hall. Returning to her desk, she prayed for strength and waited for Nanny to open the door.

Lord Osborne was a man with a purpose – impatient to have himself heard and accepted. While Nanny was closing the door, he took two long strides to where Emma sat and dropped to one knee. Taking one of her hands loosely in his own, he began, more self-conscious than she had ever seen him.

"Miss Watson, I have not been myself these many weeks. I hardly think of hunting. My horses and dogs lie idle. I am a man overcome with feelings. From the moment you caught my eye, I wished to be near you, to seek you out. I have not the gift of eloquence. Please let me say no more and agree to be my wife."

A dreadful pause for both ensued, before Emma answered, "I cannot, sir."

He hesitated for many moments, convinced he had misheard. Then with puzzled features he said, "I beg your pardon. Do you decline me?"

"I am deeply sorry, but I must decline."

Lord Osborne arose, walked to the other side of the room and, running his fingers through his already unkempt hair, turned to face her. "Do you require time, Miss Watson?"

"No, sir." She was now standing, although holding the back of the chair for support.

With some emotion, he said, "I have been led to believe that my addresses were welcome, that my offer was expected and would be accepted. Your sister Penelope … your brother Robert … I was encouraged and advised as such."

"But not by me, sir. Again, I truly regret the confusion but my answer is no, most decidedly no. If you were deceived, it was not by me. I am sorry."

It took all Emma's strength to resist the urge to run from the room at this moment. To witness the humiliation of a fellow creature was painful, and one which she was causing, excessively so. She knew, however, that he deserved, at least, her staying put and helping him to understand. This part took less time than she expected. His was not the nature to pace and rage, implore or beg. Inexperienced in such matters, he fell back on the one strength of character which saw him through many of life's challenges – his sportsmanship.

"If this is how you feel, Miss Watson, so be it. I apologise. I gave it my best but lost and now accept defeat. The misunderstanding was all on my part. I have misjudged and been sure of success where there was no reason to hope. I have made a fair attempt to win your affection and failed. Please accept my apology for any distress caused. I will leave you now."

A quick bow and he left the room, leaving Emma in a flux of emotions. It had been dreadful, as dreadful as she knew it would be. There was no middle way, no half answer she could give that would spare his humiliation or her anxiety and guilt – not only towards him but towards all her family, who she knew depended on her accepting him to promote their own hopes. She was surprised to find that mixed in with the present turmoil was a feeling of gratitude towards the gentleman she had refused. He had not made her suffer. He did not wish to punish her despite receiving an unfavourable response to his proposal. She had often thought him selfish but not now. He had retreated as abruptly as he had entered, with dignity and without undermining hers, and for this she was grateful. She could only hope and pray that Robert would react likewise on the morrow.

CHAPTER SEVENTEEN

Emma would recall that night as one of the most wretched of her life. Lying in bed she reflected on the selfish hopes of Sam, Lord Osborne's proposal, Mr Howard's loathing, the uncertain health of her father and the promise of anger and retribution from Robert on the morrow.

Her brother arrived later than expected, making the most anxious of states more difficult to bear. When at last he arrived, skipping through the door, Emma was quite ill with worry.

"Well, is it done? May I call you Lady Osborne?"

Her tired, swollen eyes and downcast expression supplied him with an answer. He halted in his step.

"Tell me you did not refuse him."

Emma, sitting with hands limply on her lap, lowered her gaze to the floor as the tirade began. Robert stormed about the room with flailing arms and risen voice. Occasionally, he lowered his flushed face so close to Emma's that she was obliged to shut her eyes. What did she think she was about? She was a disgrace to her family. What of her duty? The decision was not hers to make. His wife would cry night and day – why were his sisters so selfish? Did they not think of others? Emma would be denounced by the world as a selfish, fickle girl. With only one sister married and a father close to death, what did the other three think they were about? They had accepted her back into the family, though she was a stranger to them, and this was how she repaid them. Fourteen years was a long time and with nothing to show for it. She must have displeased the Turners for them to treat her so. That was the truth of the matter. She was undeserving and foolish, not fit to make choices on her own. Then at last, Robert asked, "What do you have to say in your defence?"

"I do not love him."

"You do not love him. *This* is why you refused him? I cannot tell you how this angers me. Love! You did not dislike him, this much I know, and that should have been enough – that he would condescend to ask one such as you, with nothing to recommend herself. I believe most women so circumstanced would have taken Lord Osborne and trusted to love after marriage."

"I shall make amends."

Robert walked to the window and with hands behind his back fell silent for many long moments before saying, "But how shall you make amends? You have nothing."

Finally, he turned around slowly and spoke in a lower, calmer tone. "I do not blame you, Emma. It was my fault, not yours. I should not have entrusted such a simple task to you. When I had learned of Lord Osborne's intention, I should not have written but come immediately that I might have overseen events and steered them to a successful and happy conclusion. Had I been more observant on our last meeting, I would have noted that your weakness of character would prevent you from performing your duty. I should have come. I would have *made* you take him."

This belittling of her capacity to think and act for herself and the manner in which it was expressed was more than Emma was willing to bear. As Robert turned to her, a look of disgust on his face, she stood up.

"I have done no wrong, Robert. You speak of duty. It is all I have known my entire life. My first wish has always been to know the peace that arises from pleasing others but I cannot accept a man I do not love. There is no greater evil than to betray oneself."

"Actually, I beg to differ. I can think of several greater evils. The workhouses, for instance, are full of wretched creatures who would agree with me. When Father dies, which may be soon, who will maintain you? I have my own family to consider. Would you steal from them? I cannot and will not provide for a gaggle of sisters. Whatever of the others, I will not support she who must marry, could marry and will not."

"But Robert," Emma pleaded, her voice shaking, "a lady without protection, with nowhere to turn, is ruined."

"Yes, she is. A fate that, in this situation, she chose."

Robert said no more. Snatching his hat from the table, he stormed from the room, slamming the door behind him.

For several hours Emma sat alone in a state of distress and numbness, the quiet of the darkening, empty room her only comfort. At least here she could be wretched uninterrupted. Finally, Nanny knocked gently on the door and entered the room to light the candles, asking if Emma would like some dinner, which she said she would not, and whether she or Emma should bring up the master's gruel. Emma, knowing that Margaret was due home at any moment, made her excuses for an early retirement and thanked Nanny for tending to her father. For the most part she did not sleep but, when she did, Robert's face appeared before her, all anger and fury. Had he been right in what he said? Was she a great disappointment and a burden to her family? She concluded that she was. Surrendering to the tears that must at last have their way, she wept aloud and mourned the absence of her beloved Elizabeth.

CHAPTER EIGHTEEN

One person who had never set foot in Stanton, though he shared many acquaintances with the Watsons and lived not far off, was Solomon Tomlinson. Unfortunately for Emma, he chose for his maiden visit the very morning after her scene with Robert, when she felt at her lowest and had hardly strength to face him. Nanny had let him in which was, as she quickly informed him, against her better judgement and grumbled at the early hour at which he called while going off to summon her mistress from upstairs. Emma met him in the hallway from whence he refused to step into the drawing-room.

"Then you have come to see my father," said Emma, "but I am afraid he is not well enough at present to see visitors."

"Oh dear me, no, I am not here to see your father, Miss Watson. I never visit the sick when I can help it. Mr Howard performs that undesirable duty in our parish. I have come instead to present you with this."

His manner was triumphant and his eyes danced as he handed her a copy of the *London Gazette*.

"I came at my earliest convenience to deliver this essential periodical for your perusal. I have purchased several copies, dispatching in order of importance – first one to Osborne Castle, next to Wickstead and finally here to Stanton that you may all read my piece entitled 'The Evils of Women Novelists'. The editor, obviously a man of great faith, saw fit to publish the letter of condemnation in full and gave it the most prominent spot, just opposite an account of the latest scandals of the royal family. I made such an argument as to the dangers of losing one's soul on reading the works of Mrs Oliver and her kind, that she shall never sell so much as a pamphlet again."

"Sir, I am sure we do not need to trouble you so, there are many others whom I am sure would appreciate this more than we at Stanton. At present, it is only my father and I here and we have hardly time or spirits for reflecting on such a solemn subject. My sister Margaret is rarely at home and none other is here so please bring it elsewhere where it will receive a greater welcome."

"The gravity with which you treat this matter and your wish to spread its message to other homes is a credit to you, Miss Watson, but as you were of the breakfast party at Osborne Castle when first I was inspired to deliver a sermon on this topic, I feel it is imperative that you receive this. My mission has become clear to me," said Mr Tomlinson, almost dropping his newspapers as he attempted to point at the Heavens, "and although I can tell you little now, know this, I shall not be swayed."

"Thank you, Mr Tomlinson. If you please, I have to tend to my father now. I can see you have several more copies to dispatch."

"Yes, indeed, I have such a day before me. Good morning."

Emma watched Solomon Tomlinson's departure in disbelief. Such arrogance and blindness ensured that he read each situation with which life presented him as only gave him pleasure. Everything benefitted and advanced his interest and what he could not explain away in some distorted manner, he would dictate that the Lord had intended it so. He could never lose. Emma wondered at how much easier life might be and how much lighter her heart, if she bore a conscience like Solomon Tomlinson's. No shame lived there, no burdens, no guilt, no constraints – a mind ever righting its own wrongs and letting the world think what it pleased – for whatever it thought, it was nothing to him.

Emma shook her head, walked into the parlour and opened the newspaper to read the dreaded article. She was only halfway through when, uttering "Insolent man" to herself, she closed it in disgust and put it under a quantity of books that sat on the shelf in the corner. She wished to burn it but decided that such was the vanity of Mr Tomlinson that he might return to learn of its fate and have his damning letter praised so, for now, she banished it out of sight and attempted to gather her strength for the day ahead.

Margaret joined Emma after breakfast and soon announced plans to spend Christmas with their cousins in Crawley. The Sandlers had been most pressing in their desire for her to join them. She was particularly intimate with one of their cousins who was quite wild for her to see the festivities they had planned and as her friends the Masons had agreed to take her, there was nothing more to it. Tom Musgrave would miss her, of course, but she was confident that the strength of his regard could withstand a short absence. Besides, there was nothing in Stanton for her. Everyone was commenting on how pale she had become – a trip to the Sandlers would restore her spirits. As her argument in favour of Crawley came to a conclusion, she noted how her being from home would mean less expense for their household and less use of the horse. Delighting in her selflessness and interpreting Emma's silence as acquiescence, Margaret ran off to pack with a good humour that was to last, at least, until her departure the following afternoon.

The household, Emma consoled herself, would become noticeably quieter and although weary of body, Emma accepted full care of her father, without objection and with the relief of one seeking distraction from their thoughts.

Another day passed and when Mr Watson's appetite could not be encouraged, Dr Richards was summoned. Following his examination of the patient, he walked slowly down the stairs shaking his head while Emma followed behind.

"What is your opinion, doctor?"

"How has he been of late?"

"Surprisingly improved up to several of weeks ago. He was up almost every day in company and his spirits were high. Now, he is quite the opposite."

"So it often is with people when they are dying. I am sorry to pain you, Emma, but it is widely known that as people approach the end of their lives, they often get a misleading gust of energy that gives false hopes to their loved ones."

Emma fought back tears.

"If he would only eat then, perhaps, I might be more hopeful. I will come again in a few weeks but send for me sooner if you must," said the doctor kindly. "And prepare yourself please. There is no need to call for your relatives just yet but if he does not improve by my next visit, that is the course of action I will be recommending. Make plans, Emma, as if the worst may happen. Be prepared."

After the physician left, Emma took her father his tea. She tried several times to press the cup to his lips until, at last, with a wave of his hand and crying *"Out vile jelly"*, he sent the cup flying across the room.

Emma knelt down to pick up the broken cup.

"Father, you must have some tea, you simply must. I have it made sweet especially." Emma wept.

"Is that you Cordelia? I am your father and a foolish old king with three daughters. I have betrayed them. What shall I do? Where is my man Gloucester that I may seek his advice?"

"I will bring you another cup soon and please, you must try, for my sake if not for your own."

"As flies to wanton boys are we to the gods. They kill us for their sport."

A tear ran down Mr Watson's cheeks. "I have lost her. There is no hope."

Emma wiped away the tear. "Please, Father, rally around. I cannot bear my burdens and if you would just rally around, I know it would aid me so much. If you would just attempt to strengthen your body and lift your spirits. I cannot do it for you."

"Thou shouldst not have been old till thou hadst been wise."

Emma sat by his bed and waited another half an hour, watching the calming effects that the laudanum, administered earlier, was having, until at last he was asleep. He had not raved like this before but such a long time without sleep and little food would, Emma reasoned, make King Lears of us all.

Leaving her father's side, Emma took her heaviest shawl and gently closing the front door so that Nanny would not realise she had taken to the outdoors again, walked to the little woodland at the back of the house. Any of the vacant rooms at Stanton would have sufficed for her contemplation but she knew that there was something about nature, perhaps its spaciousness and orderliness, which rendered her thoughts clearer.

Sitting down on a mossy stump, she determined to remain there until she could discover some way out of her misery. Her dilemma – to find a way to appease the wrong she had committed in other people's eyes without creating a greater wrong in her own. The more she pondered, the bleaker the future looked. The more frantic she became, the more likely a life of destitution appeared. These were the facts as they appeared before her now – Mr Howard despised her, she had refused Lord Osborne to the horror of her family, she was not wanted by her aunt's husband in Ireland, she had no income of her own and on her father's death, her brothers either would not or could not support her.

Thinking of Elizabeth in Chichester and reflecting on

their mutual affection, she was glad that life had shown her that a sister's love was a great consolation when other sources were absent. With some effort therefore, she calmed her mind and lessened her panic as she strived to find reasons to be hopeful. Really, she contemplated, she needed little to get by and would be of little hindrance to whatever sibling took her in. If she had not brothers to support her at least she had sisters who would – Elizabeth, the most dear among them, had promised to do so and things were looking favourable for her now in Chichester. Emma, herself, was still young and might get married in time. She could not love him, of course, if he were not Mr Howard, but if time could lessen her pain, she might eventually learn to feel regard, respect and genuine affection. Her final hopeful thought before returning to the house was that her father might surprise them all and live for many years yet.

Back indoors, Emma acknowledged that while she had not found a solution to her problem, she was less overwhelmed than formerly. Sitting down to write to Elizabeth, a knock at the front door signalled a visitor. It was Mr Tomlinson. He had, as Emma predicted, returned to enquire after his newspaper article. She rushed to pull it out from under the books and placed it on the armchair by the fire, just as Nanny opened the door to announce his entrance.

"Ah, Miss Watson, I will not stay. I was passing and wished to enquire how the residents of Stanton found my article? It is making quite the impression about town. Ah, there it is by the hearth."

Mr Tomlinson sat down in Mr Watson's armchair, fixing

a cushion behind his back and taking up his newspaper.

"Sir, I am greatly surprised that you visit us again so soon. As I mentioned yesterday, we are few and will read it at the first opportunity. Yes, I have placed it here where my father sits to read when well enough to join us but as he is quite unwell at present, it may be some time before we see him downstairs. I had just a few minutes to read over it myself and its content would indicate that you wrote it for a male readership."

"Yes, quite so, to be studied by men who would ensure its wisdom is applied to the women of their acquaintance. Where there is not a man in the house to instruct, however, ladies should read it themselves, that they may turn their backs on vice. I must advise a similar reading elsewhere. I must say my own favourite passage is when I object to ..."

Here Emma mentally retreated for a moment, dwelling on the strangeness of the person before her instead of the words he was uttering until she heard "Of course, you shall teach ..."

"I beg your pardon, sir, what did you say just now?"

"That you shall teach it to the cottagers for they do not read themselves and, in fact, being such an illiterate lot, who will never wander near a novel, I wonder why I worry for their souls at all. My sermon on sloth may be more relevant in their lives. Howsoever be the case, it is important that they understand that a great teacher, myself, is among them and, therefore, you must impress upon them, when you do your Christmas visits, the significance of this publication."

"I will teach."

"Yes, that is the spirit, Miss Emma; spread the Good Word."

"You have opened my eyes, Mr Tomlinson, by accident it has occurred but I am grateful," replied Emma, not hearing much of what he said thereafter except him likening himself to Archangel Gabriel, the Messenger. Wishing to be alone rather than encourage him further she brought the conversation to a sudden close. Emma stood up.

"You must forgive me, Mr Tomlinson, I must attend to a matter which I have just now recollected. I beg your pardon."

"I am sure it can wait," he answered, leaning back even further in the armchair. "I was about to tell you of the sermon I am next submitting for publication on the subject of sloth."

"I am suddenly unwell, sir. I feel a little feverish."

"You should have said so at once," Solomon said, quickly rising to his feet. "In that case, I had best retire but rest assured that I will return when you are fully recovered to read it to you in full. Good day."

When he had hurried from the room, Emma clapped her hands together. She had found her solution – one that would guarantee her independence.

"I will teach! That is the answer. I will be a governess."

Why had she not thought of it before? Perhaps it was because such a sinking in society would never have crossed the mind of the once presumed heiress of Claperton Park. She, who had had several governesses of her own, was forced to consider it now and gladly did so. Not long ago, she had declared to Elizabeth that she would rather teach than marry without love. How little did she think that this might come to pass? She had refused a man she did not love and with no future means of support, she must now teach. As the most respectable solution for a lady in her predicament, it would provide a satisfactory means of keeping herself while removing the need to depend on others. How wonderful to use the gift of an excellent education that had been given to her by a beloved aunt and uncle. She would teach. Had she not recently shown an ability to teach languages and found, besides, tremendous satisfaction in its undertaking?

"I will become a governess – I will find a respectable situation, teach languages, art, arithmetic, writing, the piano forte, needlework, antiquarian studies and more besides." She must act at once. She would continue to care for her father until a suitable position was found and then leave Stanton and her heartbreak of late behind her for good. Resolved, she sat down to write, not to her sister but to her aunt, requesting that she might recommend her as a governess to one of their former friends. This letter would upset her aunt but it could not be helped. She must use the best connections in her circle of acquaintance to find herself a comfortable situation, without delay.

CHAPTER NINETEEN

Emma dispatched the letter to her aunt in Ireland, laying out all her plans in a tone of confidence that she might not appear weak and pliable. Unwavering in her intentions, her aunt must know that the girl she had raised as her own and who had obeyed her every request without question, was now a woman who must make her own decisions. The letter, however, was affectionately written and indicated, in advance, an appreciation for any support her beloved relative could offer.

Stanton had not known a Christmas as quiet as the current one with only Emma and her father at home. Nanny was to spend the festive season with her sister in Guildford and James took a few days to be with his family just outside Dorking. Nanny had offered to remain at Stanton but Emma would not hear of it – the parsonage's convenient location on the edge of the village meant she had a plentiful supply of neighbours to call upon, including their cook Betty, if necessary.

A great storm broke on Christmas Eve which lasted for several days and the effects of which were felt for several more. Trees had fallen on roads and only the most foolish or necessitous of folk would attempt any movement until it had passed. Emma was grateful that she had finished all her charitable duties the week before, when there were others at Stanton, and now, with no visitors expected, she remained quiet by the fireside in the parlour, reading, or sitting with her father upstairs.

With the first post to make its way, once the roads were made accessible, a letter from Elizabeth arrived.

North Pallant Street, Chichester.

Dear Emma,

A sudden allergy to Penelope has made me embrace letter-writing with a new vigour … in fact, rather than listen to her unkind comments on the conduct and appearance of friends who have just visited this morning, I find writing to you has taken a new pressing urgency. And the difficulty is that she is often correct, for her friends are the silliest, vainest nobodies I have ever encountered, who, on first meeting me, found fault with my figure, clothing and character. Penelope dislikes them behind their backs but is the dearest, sweetest friend to their faces. Such hypocrisy, as you know, is not in my nature. Yesterday, when asked for my opinion, I told Miss Longhorn that her bonnet was too big for her face and received such a lecture from Penelope afterward. I would not have been so honest if Miss Longhorn was not so horrid. Penelope now encourages me to use the library each morning, only occasionally necessitating my presence when Lady Edgeworth calls, and assured me I will not be interrupted here.

I must be done with the most difficult part of my correspondence first. Dear Emma, prepare yourself for a great shock. It was Penelope, you know, who turned Mr Howard against you on the morning at the castle – she told me so herself. Fearing that you liked Mr Howard too much, she spoke to him when you and Lord Osborne left the drawing-room. She claimed that you enjoyed the attentions of the young nobleman and intended to accept him. Worse, I am afraid to say, she informed him that there were no secrets between sisters, that you broke his confidences several times and that we all laughed at his innocent attachment. She advised him to turn his attention elsewhere to save himself further embarrassment. I know how this pains you for, if you recall, this is how she behaved with Purvis – turning him against me. I have lectured her on your behalf and did so in front of the doctor, who agreed with me and said "Absolutely" at all the right moments. He was quite ashamed of her and she was angry with me for revealing it to him – she was out of sorts all day. I am so sorry to have to share this with you sister, you who are undeserving of such treatment and worthy of every happy feeling. It is best that you know what the wounds really are and who has truly injured you. At least it clears Mr Howard of the charge of being temperamental for no reason.

How is dear Father? Has he improved? And how is your sweet little heart? We have heard that you refused

Lord Osborne as Jane sent us word from Croydon. She said that Robert was outraged and she herself was made ill by it. I was not surprised, of course, but Penelope, I confess, was furious.

Perhaps everything will turn out well – if only we can make Mr Howard know what Penelope did. In time, you may both start afresh. I know that your meeting with Robert will have distressed you but please do not dwell on it. I will marry and, somehow, provide for us both. Believe me when I say you will not be unprotected.

I am determined, for the remainder of this letter, to rally your spirits with my important nothings. I hope it will distract you to know that our ball last evening was very thin, but by no means unpleasant, and as I had been offered three methods of getting there (the Shaws, Lady Edgeworth and Penelope) I must have been more at the ball than anybody else. Mr Shaw and I are fast becoming friends for we have discovered that there is more fun to be had if we unite in our making sport of others, which added greatly to last night's entertainment. My black cap, you will not be surprised to hear, was openly admired by Lady Edgeworth and secretly, I imagine, by everybody else in the room. Perhaps black was most appropriate, for I was mourning the absence of one of my three suitors, whose interfering uncle has relocated him to York. I had best act fast before the other two disappear in a similar fashion for Chichester is full to the brim of meddlesome and inquisitive uncles.

I am quite torn between the two who remain. Mr Phillips is a gentleman who inherited a great fortune from his aunt for taking her name before she died. Would that it were so simple for us to attain a fortune, I would not care what I was called. He is tall and thin (of person and hair) but stout of character and wealth. He is a little too fond of cards, in particular Hazard, and reputedly once played for three days without sleep, winning and losing vast sums. Dr Harding, bless him, does not feel he is good enough for me, though he is rich and respectable. He claims I would be a widow within twelve months which, if he were not to gamble away his entire fortune before then, might not be a bad thing.

The other suitor is Mr Mortimer, a steady but boring character. I now yawn less during his lengthy speeches on the military career of Lord Nelson and have resigned myself to being the wittier of us two. Penelope is keen on my liking him, for he is rumoured to be in line for a title and she had much rather refer to me, to her dreadful friends, as 'my sister, Lady such-and-such' than plain old Elizabeth. He is the handsomer of the two, however, and if one could but block out the sound of his voice, one could be made to fall in love with him. A twenty-foot dining table would remedy the problem, I believe. Mr Shaw declares that the thought of me being married to the greatest bore in England gives him an extraordinary sense of pleasure. His sister, however, feels I should not encourage either man but hold a greater value on myself. 'Value', as I informed her, is the crux of my problem but heiresses such as she, well-meaning as they are, can know little of such things.

I will write again soon and look forward to hearing all your news. Tell Nanny I have found her the brightest, most showy yellow ribbon in town. It really does pain my eyes to look upon it but I know how she loves such things so I could not leave it behind.

My love to all,
Elizabeth.

The cruelness of Penelope's interference in her affairs took Emma's breath away. It was a betrayal of every natural bond and trust, one which she did not know how she might ever forgive. The only solace from the confession was that at least she now knew the truth and that truth was that Emma had not fallen in Mr Howard's opinion but that he had been deceived by another. He had felt hurt, humiliated and betrayed based on untruths. He must know by now, however, that Penelope had lied, that she had refused Lord Osborne and yet he had not come. Despite Elizabeth's optimism, Emma alone had seen his departing look and felt that the harm that was done could not be undone. He must still believe that she had broken his confidence. So while she believed there was the slimmest possibility that over time, the truth might be revealed, it would be unwise to pin her hopes on a return to that intimacy they had formerly known. The only certainty in her life right now was that Robert had disowned her – her plans for the future must remain unchanged.

The letter also convinced Emma that it had been

best, after all, that Elizabeth had been the one to go to Chichester. Her darling sister, who had sacrificed many years as substitute mother to the family and primary carer of their father, was enjoying herself greatly and, if the letter was an accurate indicator, her dream of being wed could soon become a reality.

The following day, Emma was surprised to receive another letter from Elizabeth.

North Pallant Street, Chichester.

Dear Emma,
Please do not be alarmed, dear sister, that I write again so soon. I am afraid that the most dreadful thing has occurred to Mr Shaw. He has been gravely injured – with little hope of recovery. Though I do not show it to the others, I greatly fear for his life and regret every bad thing I have ever said of his character. Yesterday, he and the doctor were passing an incident at the market – a boy was being beaten. Mr Shaw intervened to protect the boy and was set upon by two men, one of whom stabbed him before running off. The doctor, acting fast, had him removed to this house, which is nearest. He is unconscious still and the doctor states that the next two days are critical. Penelope screeches her worries, smells salts and creates a scene in front of Louisa and her parents but when they are not here, she complains of how her trip to Bath has been postponed. She cannot abide having sickness in the house so I and the doctor are nursing him.

Solomon Tomlinson has called on us in the midst of all this chaos. He was quite put out that Mr Shaw is unconscious and close to death and, therefore, in not being alive enough to acknowledge him, he cannot call to Mr Shaw's house and meet his sister. He left very angry at the expense he has incurred in Chichester and I dare say will return bitter to Surrey without having once met with Louisa. He did one strange thing, however, he left a newspaper for us to read. What a strange fellow – as if we have time for reading newspapers at such a moment!

I will write to you again soon. Please let me know how you go. I do hope Father is well, for I feel I must stay here to be of assistance for now. Pray, remember me to everyone.

Yours affectionately,
Elizabeth

Such news! And with Mr Watson's dejected mood and Margaret not due home for another few days, Emma had no one to share it with. She marvelled at Elizabeth's ability to remain calm and practical in the midst of it.

Emma responded to her sister immediately, offering words of reassurance. At least, she noted, Mr Shaw was receiving the best attention possible and Elizabeth's assistance and experience would be a great comfort to both his family and to Penelope and the doctor. She mentioned very little regarding Penelope, knowing that the same lady might steal a look at the correspondence, if Elizabeth was not careful to conceal it. She said that she felt "greatly injured" and they could talk over it more when Elizabeth returned. She mentioned neither her father's true state of despondency nor her plans to become a governess. The former's condition she described as "unchanged" so as not to add to Elizabeth's worries. The latter she felt it best not to mention until they met in person. She had yet to hear from her aunt and, until she did, she knew that the opinions and interference of family members, even those who loved her best, could be harmful to her plans.

CHAPTER TWENTY

Emma was in the midst of looking over the household expense book in her father's study when she spied, through the window, the figure of a spritely lady approaching the house. It was Mrs Blake. She had just time to return to the drawing-room and take up her needle before the lady's entrance was announced.

They hugged on meeting and Mrs Blake was not long seated when she said kindly, "Emma, my dear, it is not easy to be a young woman. We had heard the news regarding Lord Osborne's proposal and your response. Please know, Miss Watson, that if we had not a house of sick children, I would have visited much sooner. I know that this must be a difficult time for you. There may have been talk of expectations dashed but I wished for you to be reassured that you are still a friend to all at Wickstead."

Emma gathered all her courage to ask, "And your brother is aware?"

"Yes, quite. And he would join me in these sentiments, I am sure, if he had not left suddenly on urgent business."

Emma's spirits sank and whatever morsel of hope she had held that, on learning she was now free, he would come to find her, was now gone. In her mind she dwelled on the painful facts: *he knows and yet he did not come. Instead he left. What could Penelope have said to have him hate me so?*

A difficult pause was broken by Emma acknowledging her gratitude to Mrs Blake. She had risked displeasing her friends at the castle in order to reassure her friend at Stanton and, at this very lonely time for Emma, she felt huge warmth for the lady before her. Up to now, no friends had rushed to support her and offer words of kindness.

"And tell me how your father does, dear Emma."

"I fear he is not well and does not leave his room at present."

"That is a great shame. Had you sufficient help over Christmas? You look pale. Is Nanny about and Margaret?"

"Margaret is due back any moment. She was away with friends and Nanny returned to me last Friday. It is such a comfort to have her about."

"So you were alone at Christmas. Oh Emma, that is frightful! Such a time to be on your own and yet you still have so little assistance. Is there any way I can be of use to you now?"

"No, I thank you ... but, yes, actually there is one matter where you may be the only person who can assist me."

"Tell me at once and I will do it."

"I have decided to teach, to become a governess, and I will need a letter of recommendation in order to secure a position."

Emma paused but an astonished Mrs Blake said nothing so she continued. "I have no other experience than that which I gained at Wickstead. My uncle ensured that I received a good education so I am proficient in the arts and languages among other subjects. I will require a letter of recommendation as I recall my aunt would not appoint a governess without one. Would you kindly write one for me?"

Emma was blushing as she asked, partly from mortification at being obliged to ask and partly from knowing that Mr Howard would soon know how her circumstances were changing.

"Of course I will, Emma. But why this decision? You never mentioned it before. I understand you refused Lord Osborne but you act hastily. I know Stanton will not always be your home but you have a family."

Emma's colour deepened and she looked down as she answered. "You must know we have no wealth. My sisters are in the same position as myself, excepting Penelope, and my brothers are not able to support us."

"Sam is an apprentice, but Robert must have a plan."

"And I am not part of it any longer. He may support Elizabeth and Margaret in some way but he has sworn not to assist me. He was rendered very angry by my decision not to accept Lord Osborne. I beg you, please let us not speak of it more. I wish to tell you about Elizabeth in Chichester and the terrible occurrence regarding Mr Shaw."

The conversation moved in a different direction until Margaret returned and, not realising a guest was present, rushed into the room, wide-eyed and eager to tell Emma something. She stopped suddenly in her tracks when she noticed Mrs Blake, apologised for disturbing them, curtseyed and said she must go up at once to see her father.

Mrs Blake left soon after and Emma, hearing loud voices

from her father's room, rushed up to see what all the noise was about. Mr Watson was sitting bolt upright in his bed, listening attentively to Margaret, who on hearing Emma enter, turned at once.

"How funny that Mrs Blake was here. She must not know yet but she will soon. It is the talk of the town today. Your Mr Howard and Lady Osborne are lovers."

Emma sat down on the chair next to her father's bed. "I beg your pardon?"

"They are lovers and may have been since goodness knows when. It is now assumed that they were always lovers, even while Lady Osborne's husband lived. Adulterers. How convenient for them that he died."

"Margaret, I have no idea of what you speak." Emma's stomach tightened.

"My friends, the Masons, and I stopped at The Three Cups last evening while the horses were changed. We were coming from Crawley as you know and I was most curious for there was such noise and crowds, travelling from London to Brighton and in the other direction, that there was much to see – it was all so exciting. And just before we departed, as I strained to look from our post-chaise, I saw Lady Osborne enter her carriage, turning to the gentleman with her, and they embraced, most passionately. He then mounted his grey mare and set off in the direction of London. It was Mr Howard."

"Well, I never," said Mr Watson. "The clergymen today must have a different code of conduct. We were very proper in my day."

"Margaret, this is most serious. Reputations are at stake

and, as you said, it was night time. Are you absolutely certain it was they you saw?" asked Emma.

"It was, I swear it. The Osborne family crest was on her carriage and he rode his grey mare, the exact one I saw with my own eyes when we were at the castle. And it is too late to worry about reputations for we told everyone we met with and we have called on at least six families this morning. The Tomlinsons think it a great scandal and that he is a hypocrite and sinner and she an adulteress. Mrs Rochford said she did once hear mention that her ladyship left her husband and ran off to join Mr Howard in Oxford but that she was found and dragged back to the castle. All their secrets are coming out now," said Margaret, rubbing her hands together.

Emma did not think, until now, that her aching and forlorn heart could take any more pain than it had carried of late. She was overcome. "It is over," she said to herself repeatedly. "I can never have him. He loves her." If ever there had been a hope, as Elizabeth suggested, that they could begin again, it was now crushed. His fate was tied up with another. Emma wondered if she had deceived herself that he had ever felt affection for her, or was it in fact that her "betrayal" of him had pushed him into the arms of a woman with whom he already had a strong connection? And what of the mortification that Mrs Blake and all at the castle would have to bear? What would come of it all, when he returned? If it were true, they would surely marry – as the only proper thing to do to quell the gossip and return to respectability. There was nothing to stop them, if they were inclined. He was much younger than Lady Osborne, twenty years perhaps, and she was his patroness, so in that regard gossip was assured, but what was idle talk to two persons in love?

Emma's head throbbed and she believed she could not take any more developments of this nature – betrayal, lies, deceit, gossip, maliciousness. The only relief she could find in that moment was that her father had revived somewhat and delivered a short sermon on true love but, alas, within half an hour he had sunk back down on the pillow and returned to his former mood.

Early the following Sunday morning, Margaret Watson moved about the house in the best humour Emma had witnessed thus far. She wondered had some new encouragement from Tom Musgrave occurred to effect this transformation.

"You are in exceptionally good humour this morning, Margaret."

"I am setting off for Sunday service, that is all."

"Church-going has never had such an effect on you before, sister, and besides you are too early, you live but two minutes from the church; why allow forty?"

"Because I go to service at Wickstead and it will take me at least that long to get there. Solomon Tomlinson is giving the sermon today and if what he has been saying, going about town, is anything to judge by, it will be a magnificent one. The Masons said they will meet me there. We expect a large attendance."

Emma predicted in which direction this conversation was going, but could not help saying, "The only time you heard him in church before, Margaret, you said he was the greatest bore the pulpit had ever seen."

"He has promised to give such a condemnation on adultery, deceit, intrigues, lust and all other modes of denunciation of his patroness, of course. Lady Osborne has taken to her bed, I have heard, and has not yet arisen. The guilt of such scandalous behaviour must be a great burden. The absent Mr Howard will also be sullied but it is always the woman, don't you know, who must carry the greater share of shame."

"How dare he? A public condemnation to Mr Howard's own congregation? He attempts to humiliate them without all the facts being known. Mr Howard has not returned for matters to be clarified or to defend himself. It is an act of malice and Mr Tomlinson had best look into his own past before casting stones at others."

"I wonder why you defend them so. They have done you no great favours. Besides, if something is spoken about generally, it must be true. I intend to comfort dear Tom Musgrave when next I meet him as the shock of this impropriety will affect him greatly. We must make the most of every opportunity. I am off now, sister, I will be back as fast as I can and will tell you all."

Emma wished to inform Margaret of how ashamed of her she was and how ugly she found her delight in the misfortunes of others. Knowing, however, that it would affect no change in the culprit, she held her tongue. Instead she found Nanny and asked, "Has there been post today, Nanny?"

"None indeed my dear girl but when did we last receive a letter on the Sabbath? Hadn't I told you I would bring it to you directly, if there were?"

"Yes, Nanny. I am impatient for a letter from my aunt,

that is all. I had expected greetings and news of her at Christmas."

"She'll be busy with her new house and servants and all the goings on at Christmas. She will write to you soon, I dare say."

Emma nodded but secretly worried that her aunt had dismissed her plea for support and wondered whether the great distance between them had also lessened her aunt's regard for her and interest in her affairs.

CHAPTER TWENTY-ONE

Emma began to lose track of days as she learned that, for those who suffer, time becomes something to be endured, not relished. No visitors arrived to enliven her mornings nor did any unexpected circumstance occasion a change in her routine. She hoped for news from Chichester regarding Mr Shaw or a letter from Ireland indicating that support was available to her. Just over a week after obtaining the last correspondence, Emma received another letter from Elizabeth in Chichester. She opened it hurriedly, praying that it would bear good news with regards to Mr Shaw's health. Fortunately, it did.

North Pallant Street, Chichester.

Dearest Emma,
I am so relieved to inform you that Mr Shaw is now out of danger. He sits with me here in the study, reading, even as I write this to you. We retire to this room each morning after breakfast — me, wishing to avoid Penelope's friends, and he to make a nuisance of himself, but we do enjoy much talk and laughter — the servants are obliged to call us several times to

luncheon. He is not well enough to return home yet but sufficiently well to be out of bed for most of the day.

I am glad that it has turned out so, for I was exceedingly tired sitting by his bed each day waiting for him to become conscious or take his leave of us. The morning he awoke, he spied me by the bedside and called out, "What angel is this? I must have died," but a dart of pain brought him back to the present. I ran to fetch the doctor who said he was not out of danger until he examined his wound, and leaning him forward in the bed asked me to stay and told Mr Shaw to brace himself for a pain he would never feel the likes of again. Just as I reached to take his hand that he might have something to give him strength, he was likewise reaching out for mine. I believe that it meant something to him to have me there, for I appeared exceedingly calm and courageous, though I was trembling inside. I saw such pain cross his face but he only cried out once and the doctor declared that although there was no infection, his recovery would be slow, for the wound was deep.

What a fuss Penelope made to her husband when she heard Mr Shaw must stay. Hers, she declared, was the most generous nature. She would not hear of a man, seriously wounded, returning to his own home to recuperate. It was quite out of the question. Nobody had suffered since the incident as she had, with people popping in day and night and the prospect of a man dying under her roof. But it was all very unfair. She had let a house in Bath and it had been sitting idle, this week already. The Fosters had expected her and they would be greatly disappointed as they had missed half the season at this stage. An injury to their connection might be impossible to recover from. She felt she needed the restorative properties of the spa waters, to calm her nerves after what she had been through. To humour her, Dr Harding agreed that they would depart for Bath on Tuesday se'nnight, if Mr Shaw were sufficiently recovered to return to his home and I might leave for Stanton on the same morning.

It is peculiar but I was saddened to hear that we would part so soon. In truth, the injury has tamed Mr Shaw, even if it be but for a short time, and we are different, less severe – and while it may not be tenderness, a kinder consideration of the other's feelings has arisen. "Friendship" may be the word I am looking for, so I must needs find a new recipient for my contempt. I am starting to find that this is my favourite time of the day, in my favourite room and with my preferred company! He teaches me so much of what he has seen on his travels – of Rome, Greece, Bohemia and Moravia, and talks so brilliantly of the animals that he studies – I am quite enchanted. He will be leaving for Vienna soon for an important study he must undertake there.

We do laugh a great deal, for wit is the cornerstone of our conversation. The following is one such example,

Mr Shaw – "So Solomon Tomlinson came to call on me and was infuriated that I did not wake out of my state of unconsciousness to take tea with him. The *audacity of the man! He is determined to get my sister. Fate, that marvellous orchestrator of events, knows best how to avoid the likes of him and threw me, no doubt, in the way of a dagger to get me out of the meeting."*

Myself – "If fate was so benevolent, it would have thrown Mr Tomlinson in your stead."

I would not speak so in front of another gentleman as it may be interpreted as unkind but Mr Shaw does not seem to mind.

Enough of my adventures! I have been selfish in not asking after Father sooner. Please let me know how you fare and whether Margaret is doing her share of duties. Our patient, Mr Shaw, is to remain at home tomorrow evening as we attend a dinner party at Lady Edgeworth's house, therefore my next letter should indicate if either of my two prospective husbands has dropped to his knee (for I must bring this marriage business to a successful close as soon as possible). I confess that I do have conflicting feelings about leaving Chichester – I have had such a time of it, but coming home to you is the greatest consolation I cling to.

With sincere love to all at Stanton,
Elizabeth

The letter contained so much to delight and concern Emma that she felt compelled to read it three times over. Her beloved, lively, kind Elizabeth would be home to her soon and she wondered how she had survived these past months without her sister's comforting presence. The letter also hinted, however, at a change in sentiment towards Mr Shaw. Could Elizabeth be falling in love? This troubled Emma who, convinced as she was of the irresistible virtues of her sister, knew the hopelessness of expecting a change of sentiment in that gentleman – Mr Shaw would never marry.

CHAPTER TWENTY-TWO

Despite the promise of Elizabeth's return, Emma struggled to keep in good spirits. She had received no response from her aunt and her father's health was deteriorating. Mr Watson was due a visit from Dr Richards and Emma feared the worst as there had been no visible improvement in him, body or spirit, since the doctor's last visit.

Another matter which played greatly on her mind was that of Mr Howard and Lady Osborne. She owned that it was natural that she should be saddened by his rejection of her and tormented by intruding thoughts of his intimacy with Lady Osborne yet she could not help but feel sorry for the very public shaming they were forced to endure. Emma still held Mr Howard in high regard and hated to think how he suffered during this current scandal. Having herself so recently felt all that attends the disapproval and judgement of others, the feeling of being abandoned by those who one had considered allies meant she could relate, in some small way, to their predicament. Even Lady Osborne, who had reputedly received his love and, therefore, was, in some sense, her rival, was to be pitied – would she, who had suffered so much cruelty at the hands of her late husband, crumble under the humiliation?

One day, on returning from visiting her friends, Margaret sat curled up on the window seat and declared to Emma that despite Mr Howard's return the previous week, Osborne Castle remained in an uproar.

"Lady Osborne continues to keep to her bed. How undignified!"

"Margaret, please, have some compassion."

"Dr Richards is quite worn out from tending to her. Lord and Miss Osborne never leave the castle – from shame, no doubt – and there is still no sign of Tom Musgrave."

Emma remained silent.

"Solomon Tomlinson, to whom you have been most unkind Emma, if I do say so, continues to condemn them from the pulpit. Do not look at me like that, Emma. And why should he not when Mr Howard remains locked up in his study. Heathen man! The bishop should be informed."

"Despicable gossip. I cannot listen to another word."

"Then you will not wish to hear that Mr Howard also has a mistress in London. That is what is said about town. He visits her regularly and that is why he has not proposed to Lady Osborne."

Emma stood up and hastily left for her bedroom, where she sat upon her bed and waited for her colour and heartbeat to return to normal.

What to think? The only proper and honourable thing was for Mr Howard to propose to Lady Osborne when he returned from his trip. If they were indeed lovers, this would be a welcome and expected outcome, which would lend relief to their loved ones and allow the entire matter to blow over. Why did he not act? Why would he abandon Lady Osborne thus and distress her so? Could it be true that there was yet another lover? At the end of fifteen minutes spent in anxious contemplation, Emma arose and declared to herself that the gossip could not be entirely true, that something would yet come to light to clarify matters and that Mr Howard was still, in her opinion, the best and most honourable of men.

"If there was only something I could do. I must let them know that I bear no ill will and I will not stand by while others cast stones."

She concluded at last that she would go at once to Mrs Blake to publicly demonstrate her support, as Mrs Blake had done for her, following Lord Osborne's proposal. What was more, she would write Mr Howard a letter so that he too, despite their personal history, would know that he had one friend at least. Deciding to act in the moment while her purpose was strong, she wrote,

Stanton,

Dear Sir,
Please find herein, the map of the stars of the southern hemisphere which I had once promised you. I came upon it today and wish for you to have it for I know you will keep it safe. I understand that you go through a difficult time at present. Please know that your friends at Stanton think of all at Wickstead and offer our support.

Turn to your faith, sir, for as you once pointed out to me – We are not alone when we walk in the dark.

Yours respectfully,
Miss Emma Watson

Her resolve was to act immediately. She would walk to Wickstead. It was late afternoon – too late for visiting but her purpose made her forget such trivial formalities. They must know they had a friend in her.

Mrs Blake, observing Emma approach the house, went to the door herself to meet her.

"Miss Watson!"

"Mrs Blake, please, I do not wish to intrude on you. I have caught you off guard. It is an unusual hour to call and I must return directly for we dine early."

"Oh please do come in and rest. You cannot return so soon, not having sat or taken refreshments. I am so glad to see you, Emma."

Emma moved to the parlour with her friend with an insistence that she could remain but a minute.

"I will call again soon, you have my promise. But today, in the midst of all I hear and the anxious situation you may find yourself in, I felt compelled to call and offer my support as you did for me some weeks back."

"I thank you from my heart," responded Mrs Blake, pressing Emma's hand. "We are much obliged to you. I must confess we have had no visitors since the news broke and, therefore, I felt it unwise to call on people myself. The villagers have stopped calling to my brother. I believe they are confused as to what is the correct thing to do. Mr Tomlinson has warned them so."

Emma said all that was right without prying and Mrs Blake's gratitude and anxiety were, in equal measure, evident. Emma handed her the letter and map for Mr Howard, with the instruction not to disturb him now but to give it to him when she had left. Mrs Blake thanked her again and said she hoped that they could meet soon, perhaps when Elizabeth had returned.

As Emma walked past Mr Howard's study, she thought she heard the scrape of a chair, and as she made her way from the house to the gate, she was convinced she was being watched from his study window. Not turning around to discover for sure, she increased her pace in the direction of home.

CHAPTER TWENTY-THREE

D r Richards arrived at Stanton an hour late, blaming the necessity of meeting his apothecary at the White Hart for the delay. Enquires made downstairs into the condition of his patient prepared him to find an unresponsive and motionless man in bed. Emma had explained how troubled her father had been on occasion and how he had believed himself to be King Lear. Requesting that Emma assist him with leeching, the doctor was astonished to find, on entering the sick chamber, Mr Watson sitting up in bed, neither delusional nor despondent, eagerly awaiting his arrival. He became even more alarmed by the topic of conversation.

"I dare say, Dr Richards, you know all about Lady Osborne and her young lover. These trends come from London, do they not? Such liaisons do not occur in the countryside."

The physician smiled. "Indeed, you are mistaken, Mr Watson, I believe we are quite as guilty of such to-do as the Londoners but perhaps we do not advertise it as much."

"No, I disagree. It begins in London but catches on elsewhere and given our proximity to town, it is little wonder it has come this way at last. Mark my words, they will all be at it now."

Emma, surprised at her father's want of delicacy and his obvious enthusiasm for such a low subject, looked away.

"Sir, I must remind you that you are not at the card-table now. Your daughter is present and perhaps we had best move from the subject."

"I am a clergyman and where matters of sin and morals are concerned, I must be free to speak as I find and, indeed, I am not finished. I have only just begun."

"Father, please, let us talk of something else. It is all I hear from Margaret and I had rather thought you too ill to expend your energy so. You did not speak ten words all week and now you are all flushed and excited. Please, do not continue."

Mr Watson proceeded enthusiastically, "As I was about to say, Nanny has told me that you were at the castle this afternoon, doctor, having been called thither by Lady Osborne. Is it not true? You must have news."

Emma considered quitting the room but while her agony was great, her curiosity was greater. She stayed to hear what the doctor might say.

"What of my professional code of confidentiality, Mr Watson?"

"You have our word, doctor, we will keep it confidential. So what say you? Your silence speaks much … Then it is true what the servants say, there is an engagement!"

"Well, you will know soon enough. Yes, Lady Osborne and her young lover are engaged to be married. There is an atmosphere of jubilation at the castle."

"Then, why did they wait until now?" asked Emma, as much to herself as to the doctor.

"The young man only returned from his trip and was quite unaware of the rumours. They have made their relationship publicly known and will soon be wed. He is the happiest man I have ever met. He almost shook my hand entirely off my wrist."

Emma sank into the chair. Mr Howard was happy, delighted to become engaged to Lady Osborne. In the midst of her pain, however, a slither of relief shone through – at least it was official now. This would hasten her need to leave as soon as possible. She must never meet him again.

Mr Watson clapped his hands jubilantly. "And why should she not marry again? Every person deserves love and companionship. I am pleased for them. I will send my congratulations to them both immediately. I will dictate. Emma, you shall write for me."

"Father, I do not ..."

"Emma, I insist. My writing slope is on the shelf. In it you will find paper and ink. Go there to your mother's small table and we shall begin."

Emma removed the writing slope from the shelf and, pushing some of his books aside, made just enough room on the desk to place it. When the tools were ready and with tightened chest, she whispered, "I am ready, Father."

"Very good. Let us begin with the fortunate husband-to-be. Are you ready, Emma?"

"Yes, Father."

"Good, then let us commence. *Stanton* and today's date, though I do not know what it is. You may fill it in yourself, my dear. What date is it?"

"February 1st."

"Let us begin again then. *Stanton, February 1st. Dear Sir. It is with the utmost delight* ... Do I speak too fast my dear?"

"No, Father, you speak at the correct speed." Emma coughed to hide the emotion in her voice.

"It is just that you looked forlorn. I thought you were out of patience with me."

"No, Father, I am well. Let us continue."

"Very well ... *Stanton, February 1st. Dear Sir* ... Oh, perhaps I should give him his name, it is more personal, do you not think, Emma, that it is a more friendly way to address a person?"

"Yes, I believe it is."

"And so we may begin again. We will be done in no time. *Stanton, February 1st. Dear Mr Howard. It is with the greatest –*"

"What do you mean, Howard?" the doctor interrupted, with leech held mid-air. "You have the wrong man. Have you not heard? It is Tom Musgrave whom she marries."

"I beg your pardon, doctor, you are mixing the two young men up. It is Howard who she weds."

"No, Mr Watson. I assure you that I know for certain. It is Tom Musgrave. Yes, there was some rumour circulating that it was Howard at the inn but it was in fact Tom Musgrave. It was he who was leaving from the inn that evening. He rode on Howard's grey mare, for his own horse was lame. That was all. It was enough, of course, for a false rumour to begin. It was and is Musgrave whom you must congratulate.

He has finally got his foot in the door of Osborne Castle and the rest of him has followed suit."

Emma, who was leaning over the letter, now stared blankly at the doctor before sinking back in her chair.

"Well, I never! Indeed. What! Emma, we were quite wrong by Howard and his intrigues. I must say as much to Margaret and read her some lectures on spreading false tidings. Indeed! Well, well. Still, I am glad she is to wed again, though I prefer Howard any day to Musgrave."

"There are no obstacles – financial or otherwise," said the doctor, closing his medicine bag. "There is but the issue of age – almost twenty years."

"Ah, but Shakespeare, like Tom Musgrave, married a lady many years older than himself and if it is good enough for the greatest of men, why not for the greatest of rascals," said Mr Watson, rubbing his hands together.

"You are quite sure, doctor? It is Mr Musgrave and not Mr Howard?" asked Emma.

"Absolutely."

Dr Richards suggested aloud that he and Emma leave Mr Watson to rest. When downstairs, Emma wished to continue her questions regarding the engagement, but without her father, any return to the subject seemed ill-timed.

The doctor shook his head while putting on his coat to leave.

"He confuses me, Emma."

"And I, doctor. This past week, he has had occasional frenzies like this but otherwise he lies there, like he has given up on life."

"From what I see today, it is difficult to know what to do. He is weak, his heartbeats are irregular, his rheumatism is agitated, he suffers from lack of appetite and excessive fatigue, but his actual ailments and pains are what they ever were. Then he has moments of heightened excitement and lucid talk. I do not know what to advise."

"Shall I summon my brothers and sisters and maybe our friend Mrs Ellingham?"

"Perhaps it is best; let them come, not all at once, but gradually so that he does not suspect. I will have to review him again next week. This may be a phase – it will have to come to an end sooner or later, for better or worse. All I can do in the meantime is observe and make him comfortable."

Emma thanked the doctor but was glad to see him leave. She needed quiet to contemplate what she had heard regarding Mr Howard. If the doctor had checked her pulse then, he would have found it most irregular too. Tom Musgrave was to marry Lady Osborne. They were lovers and he had just returned from his trip. This explained why Mr Howard had not acted; in fact, nobody could act, until Tom Musgrave returned. One moment's thought was given to Margaret who, on visiting the Masons to hear the latest gossip, would surely have received the blow by now. Her beloved Tom Musgrave favoured another.

But the main point on which Emma could not but dwell over and over was that Mr Howard was innocent in conduct and more significantly, he was free. And though it did not alter his opinion of her, she could not but rejoice in the fact that he had not been deceiving her. There had been no third party – he had most likely felt something, as she had, all that time they had spent together. This brought comfort in the moment. A dull regret lingered, however, at the thought that had it not been for Penelope's interference, things might have turned out differently for them. She could not afford to dwell for long on her own concerns for there was something urgent to attend to at once. She must sit down and undertake the difficult task of writing to Robert, Sam, Penelope and Mrs Ellingham, indicating that a visit to see Mr Watson was advised. Within a few days, Emma received a response from Mrs Ellingham to inform her that she would arrive as soon as the next possible mode of transport could bring her.

CHAPTER TWENTY-FOUR

Emma had begun to cease blaming recent storms, Christmas preoccupations and jealous husbands for the fact that she had not yet received a response from her aunt and convinced herself that she must plan for a future without her support, regardless of the sadness that this thought brought her. She had yet, among her papers, the address of a former and favourite governess and was resolved to write to her seeking advice, when the letter from Ireland finally arrived.

Cloonliss, Ireland

My dearest darling Emma,
I do hope this letter reaches you before you have taken any sudden actions on your plans, as outlined to me in your letter, which was a great shock to me. Please forgive the delay in writing it but I needed to hold off until I had some news.
I confess that I was distraught that my girl, my pride and joy since she was five years old, whom I raised as my own daughter, would be reduced to seeking employment as a governess. This is not what your

uncle and I had wished or hoped for you and I could not help but wonder what he would think of it, if he knew. It does not honour his memory to contemplate it or how my own actions contributed to your decision.

In a state of distress, I summoned my husband who, though he be a hard man in some respects, is not a wicked man. He listened attentively to my concerns and my request that he would make some provision for you in the sale of Claperton Park. It had not been his intention, as he finds himself quite in debt at his Irish estate so at first he refused. How foolish I have been, my dear, with regard to you. I should have secured your independence when it was within my power to do so. Forgive me, my dear, for I find it difficult to forgive myself. Know that your aunt is extremely happy with the Captain and is treated as any lady could hope to be treated but the matter preyed greatly on my spirits and at last, he conceded to £1,500 on the sale of Claperton Park. It will be necessary to wait for a time, as the whole thing may take six months or more to go through. This sum will only give you an annuity of £50 per year – not enough to live on, but if you were to reside with family you would make do. With youth and beauty on your side, I am sure you will marry a respectable man, who may take you for such a modest sum.

May I beg you again to reconsider becoming a governess? If things turn out badly with your father's health and you must leave Stanton, please contact me immediately and I will find you a comfortable *arrangement as a lady's companion, for many of my old friends would delight in having one such as you by their side. Such a respectable position would provide protection, a home and a small allowance which is by far preferable to living with a family as a governess, for with your sweet nature and innocence, I fear the worst. Who knows among whom you may be thrown and what evils may occur? Write back at your earliest convenience.*

I do hope your father's health rallies and be sure to give my love to your family.

With fondest best wishes,
Your loving Aunt O'Brien

This letter was wonderful. Her aunt's silence until now had convinced Emma that nothing was to come from her relative in Ireland and how happy she was to be proved wrong. The reminder of what might have been hers was eclipsed by the knowledge that her aunt had secured her something, however small, which would preserve her from the worst fate. She might have to wait to receive it but the promise alone made her flush with pleasure. For now, at last, she had options. She could be selective in what situation she chose, for it was still her intention to become a governess.

Fifty pounds per year was little, certainly not enough to live independently. It would not afford the rent on even the most modest of dwellings but to one who had nothing, not a shilling to her name, it was a fortune. It meant that if she wed, a more attractive bride in her modest affluence than before, she was bringing something with her into the marriage. If she did not and were to live out her life in the home of a sister or brother, she would not have to beg charity of them in order to be kept.

The idea of becoming a lady's companion, however, did not appeal. To merely provide company and conversation for a lady of wealth seemed to her an idle occupation and, worse, a punishment. She knew her aunt's suggestion was well-meaning, but she fervently hoped it was one which she would never be forced to take up.

She could now face Elizabeth, in a few days and tell her with ease of her plans for the future and feel, in her heart, that she was an heiress to an inheritance once more.

CHAPTER TWENTY-FIVE

I t was now Monday and as Elizabeth was due to arrive on Wednesday, Emma was amazed to receive, that morning, an unexpected correspondence from her sister and smiled that she had quite possibly received, in the past few months, more letters from Elizabeth than in the fourteen years she had lived away at Claperton Park. Curious to know what could have prompted her sister to write when she was due home in the immediate future, Emma opened the letter with haste.

North Pallant Street, Chichester.

My dearest Emma,
I hope you do not mind sharing the name "dearest" for I now have one as dear to me as you. It is a remarkable story, which I will recount in great detail, that you may tell your children's children. So please be seated and I will begin.

In the first instance, I hope it is not too great a shock for you when I confess that I have developed such a strong attachment to Mr Shaw during these past weeks. You may recall I mentioned in my last correspondence that we were to attend Lady Edgeworth's dinner party while Mr Shaw stayed at home. When I was finally reunited with my two impatient and enthusiastic suitors, however, I tossed them both aside – for what were they to Mr Shaw? I had lost all interest in pleasing them, flattering their taste in cravats or pretending I cared a jot for Lord Nelson, and spent the entire evening, instead, wondering what Mr Shaw was doing at that moment and whether he thought of me. But in reminding myself, on the journey home, that it was a hopeless case as he had sworn never to marry, I became increasingly annoyed with him. When he met us at the door, therefore, I hardly spoke one word and instead marched past him and retired to bed.

I became more withdrawn and cool each day – not that I could feel less for him, but it was my useless attempt to protect myself against the heartbreak I knew was coming. He became more cheerful with time and on our final morning in the study together, even joked that I had not caught either of my two men. The insensitivity of this comment and his absolute lack of awareness of the situation in hand angered me. My response was cruel – that had he not walked into a dagger, I might have had a husband by now. He started. It was unfair of me to blame him but there was some truth in what I said and it was that which affected him. He was surprised and perhaps even injured by it. I moved to the window, as the tears were beginning to come and I did not wish him to see them. We were silent a while, then he thanked me again for the kind care I had given while he was unwell and said he was now leaving to pack. I did not respond and try as hard as I could, I failed to keep the tears in any longer. Suddenly he was behind me and I will now transcribe faithfully what was said (but forgive me, as I am in love and may have only heard what I chose to hear).

"Miss Watson, do you cry? Please do not, come now, please. It was cruel of me to tease you so. I am sorry."

I turned to face him.

"I dread not seeing you, Mr Shaw, and it breaks my heart so. Now, I must begin my search again, for a man that will love me and want me as his wife and it shall be very hard as long as I think of you."

Later, Mr Shaw told me that he was truly amazed. He had always believed that he knew what he wanted, that he had wished to remain ever aloof from the needs and wants of others, to remain in control of his own life and an independent spirit. I, who he preferred to any other woman of his acquaintance, had feelings for him and brazenly spoke of them now and if he could but be honest with himself, he would know that the feeling of triumph, at keeping me from my suitors, was felt because he was jealous. He had never known such a time of happiness in his life as these months and particularly these past weeks. Everything that he boasted and professed to feel about marriage collapsed in front of him – for what could stand up to such beauty and honesty? He had thought he did not want a companion but then, he had not known Elizabeth Watson – a woman unlike any other he had met before.

"I will be that man, if you will have me."

I did not believe him and told him so.

"I swear it, Elizabeth. I wish to call you my own, if you would have me. Please. Please say you will."

I still did not believe him, so he took me by the arms and looking into my face said,

"Elizabeth – you spirited, outspoken woman – what have you done to me these past weeks? You have taken up residence in my soul, without me knowing it, and now I cannot think of another man having you. Elizabeth – my most beloved, my same me, please, say 'yes'."

And how, my dear Emma, could I possibly say "no" to such a proclamation? We decided on the spot that we must marry as soon as possible so I may join him in Vienna. Oh Emma, I have never known happiness that compares to this feeling. How could I have believed myself in love with Purvis? It was nothing to this. We waited until dinner that evening to break our news to our hosts, though we were laughing and giggling like children all day. I must say, I do not know which of the two was more astonished, for Penelope's mouth remained open and looked as if it might never shut again while all the doctor's best words had abandoned him, for though he spoke, he made no sense. Their spell in Bath will, no doubt, aid them in becoming accustomed to the idea and I hope they find, in us, the love and support of family living nearby (but fortunately, in my opinion, not in too close proximity). And once we return to England, dear Emma, you will *always have a home with us, of that be reassured. You and I shall play duets appallingly, drink tea all day and cut out dozens of ugly silhouettes.*

I am to leave in the morning but am rushing this letter off now that it should reach you a couple of days before I arrive. Do not tell my news at Stanton for I wish to see their faces when they hear that it is Mr Shaw whom I am to wed.

All the love in the world, from me to you,
Elizabeth

This was the news Emma most wished to hear and adding it to the promise she had already received from her aunt, Emma sat for half an hour laughing and crying with gratitude and relief. She had not realised how weary she was, feeling old beyond her years – exhausted in body and spirit and tired of worrying for herself and others. This letter contained so much. Elizabeth was happy. Elizabeth was to wed the man she loved and would live without fear of poverty and what is more, she had offered Emma a home for the future. Emma did not waver in her scheme to become a governess. She could now console herself, however, that were her circumstances to become difficult, there was one home where she would be welcome, where her presence was not felt as a burden. This happy thought proved an immense relief. It was as if she had been holding her breath since Robert's rejection of her and now she could breathe again. She was safe.

CHAPTER TWENTY-SIX

The moment a glowing Elizabeth set foot in Stanton, Emma ran to meet her and threw her arms around her sister. Elizabeth appeared none the worse for the exertion of her travels and consequently was pleased to be home at last and was glad to sit by her own fireside and exchange news with her sister. Nanny had left their tea beside them and following a hasty enquiry as to the health of their father, who was now sleeping, and the whereabouts of Margaret, who was now locked in her room, the two shared all that had happened since Elizabeth was last at home.

"So it was Tom Musgrave, after all. How astonishing! I had once thought he might attempt to win the heart of Miss Osborne – not her mother. But to some, I expect, Lady Osborne is preferable. She certainly is the kinder and more attractive of the two. Margaret must be outraged."

"Yes she is, poor thing. She has only once left her room since her learning of it and that was to tell me that the Masons are taking her to Croydon on Sunday, where she will stay with Robert and Jane until she finds a husband. All my attempts to comfort her have been in vain. She has sworn that she will not set foot in Stanton again until she is wed."

"I wish her some of my luck in that endeavour for I do recall that was my hope on going to Chichester and look how wonderfully well it worked out. I am to marry the last man on earth I believed I would marry and I could not be happier. But tell me, how is Mr Howard? Mr Shaw said he was innocent from the start – how delighted he is to be right."

"I could not tell you. Nanny said that he has returned to performing his parish duties and that Lady Osborne has ordered Solomon Tomlinson to leave."

"As it should be."

"Thank you for telling me about Penelope's interference, though I do not know when I shall forgive her. I can hardly bring myself to write to her at present. It is a comfort to know, however, that Mr Howard turned against me because of her malicious falsehood rather than hating me based on his own opinions. Though it alters little, it means that he did not change his mind about me but rather had his mind changed for him. I will attempt to forget him, I promise I will. Time, I feel, and distance, will be my greatest aids in that regard."

"Yes, this agony you feel I once felt over Purvis and as a result of the very same act of malice. You may yet meet Mr Howard and the misunderstanding being resolved, become friends. Then, who knows what may happen? Or you may, in time, fall in love with another. Look how I have found love again and am loved back. For these past many weeks, I have abused Mr Shaw in public but admired him in private.

Once we are married, I may abuse or admire him whenever I please. But what more news from you?"

Emma smiled broadly.

"Why, I must tell you of an inheritance of £1,500 I am to receive on the sale of Claperton Park and of my plans to become a governess."

"Emma, really! Is this true? An inheritance?" asked Elizabeth, sitting forward in her chair and taking Emma's hand.

"Yes. I am so pleased."

"How wonderful, Emma! However, I do not approve of your teaching."

"Well, you must approve of it, for I am quite determined."

"Not you – you were brought up to be a fine lady, not a governess."

"Nothing remains of the fine lady but her manners and education. And these, which she is fortunate to have, she must put to use to ensure her security and independence."

"I will not hear of it. While Father still has the house, you may live on here in Stanton, and when we return from Vienna, you must live with us, though I am sure you will be well married by then."

"Dearest Elizabeth, when you wrote that I may live with you I laughed and cried with relief. There is no one with whom the burden of dependence would be less felt. You would want me; the others would resent my presence. It may come to pass that I live with you someday but for now I must prepare for employment. It is the arrangement I prefer."

"Oh my, we must speak more of this. So much has

happened in my absence which you have not told me. I find myself unexpectedly short for words. Has anything else occurred which I should know of? Has Nanny become a pirate and James run off with a countess? Speak at once."

Just at that moment, a knock on the door signalled a visitor. Both ladies fell silent and turned to see who Nanny would admit and were alarmed to find it was Mr Howard. His manner was embarrassed and quiet, not the assertive anger Emma had witnessed on their last meeting. He held a letter in his hand and, waving it slightly, remained by the door instead of walking properly into the room.

"I bring a letter from my sister for Miss Emma." He waved it again and cleared his throat. "It is, I believe, a note of recommendation which you asked of her."

Emma, red-cheeked, stood up. "Yes, sir, why, I thank you. Please come and join us. We have just this minute brought in the tea."

Looking unsure whether to stay or go, he hesitated until Elizabeth stood, saying, "I have just now arrived from Chichester, Mr Howard. I bring the warmest regards of all in your acquaintance there, in particular Mr Shaw, who is, you may be surprised to hear, my betrothed. We have discovered that we were quite mistaken in hating each other and have decided to remedy the error with marriage."

Mr Howard's face relaxed into a smile and, shaking her hand warmly, he said, "My heartiest congratulations. Well, well, I had not expected it. I am delighted, as will my sister be when I inform her."

"Thank you, Mr Howard, thank you, and if you do not mind, I have not yet seen my father and am anxious to do so. Please be seated, I will not be long."

Elizabeth gave Emma one good-humoured, meaningful look in response to the nervous one she received and left the couple to an episode of awkward tea-pouring, tea-spilling and conversation regarding the weather.

"We have never had such a mild winter," stated Mr Howard.

"I believe you are correct."

"Excepting that bad storm over the Christmas season but otherwise extremely mild."

"Yes."

"We lost two of our apple trees during the storm."

Emma nodded.

"So mild, in fact, that the blossoms came out early."

"Yes, my father noted that also."

"He has been well enough to walk up to your orchard?"

"No, no, he has not left the house. He observed that the blossoms, in general, had come out early. He had seen some from his window."

"Why, yes, of course. I was referring to blossoms on the apple trees."

Emma smiled and lowered her gaze, but not knowing in what capacity he was visiting, dared not lead the conversation.

Mr Howard stood up and sat down twice and finally remembered to pass to Emma the letter he had crumpled in his hand.

"My sister tells me you are to tutor."

"Yes, I feel I must. It is one of the more pleasant options before me."

"She mentioned your decision was in response to your brother Robert."

"Yes, at first it was."

"He was angry, I suppose. Angry that you refused ... that you refused Lord Osborne, I dare say."

"Yes, he was."

A short pause followed, then Mr Howard, on clearing his throat, said, "Miss Watson, I cannot tell you –"

Suddenly, the door swung open and Elizabeth called, "Mr Howard, I fear the worst. Father is agitated in the extreme and has asked to speak to a clergyman immediately. Alone! Please go to him at once. I will show you to his room."

"Of course."

Elizabeth returned and the sisters sat in silence, each holding the other's hand and attempting to withhold tears.

At last, Mr Howard returned and, smiling at the sisters, said, "Go to your father. He wishes to speak with you."

CHAPTER TWENTY-SEVEN

The sisters and Mr Howard walked into Mr Watson's room and stood around his bedside. He had sunk deep into his pillows, his eyes half-closed and his lips dry. Elizabeth lifted his head gently and put water to his lips. He sipped and, after a moment, waved that he had had enough.

"Father, we are here. Emma, Mr Howard and I are here. What is it you wish to say to us?"

"Ah, Elizabeth, is it you? I have a troubled mind but this fine young man has persuaded me that I must speak freely with my daughters."

"Speak so, Father."

With emotion, Mr Watson began, "Girls, I have been a bad father. I have not provided for you as I would have wished. The living here must go to another clergyman when I die and you must find shelter with your brothers or with Penelope."

"Please do not let these things worry you. You have been, I mean, you are a wonderful parent and we could not have wished for a more loving one. Do not trouble your mind with such thoughts."

"But I have three unmarried daughters living, without an inheritance between them, under my roof. How can I not worry, when this is so?"

"Oh Father, I can relieve your mind on that score," said Elizabeth, "so do not trouble yourself a moment longer. In a very few weeks, when he is well enough to travel, you will have Mr Shaw arrive in order to ask for your consent to marry one of your daughters. The strange part is that it is I who he wishes to marry, and stranger still, I wish to marry him back. So you see, one daughter has been taken off your hands. She will travel a little but then return to live a comfortable life in Chichester and can offer a home to any of her sisters who may need it. Is this not wonderful news?"

Mr Watson sat up a little in his bed. "Can this be so? Is it true? Why, Elizabeth, I am so happy to hear it. You are quite sure that you love him?"

"Yes, Father, we are deeply in love."

"I also have something to tell you," said Emma. "I am to receive an inheritance of £1,500 from my aunt. So you see, Father, I too will be provided for."

"Help me sit up, please, Mr Howard, so that I can comprehend all this news. Well, well, Emma, this is marvellous news indeed. You will all be safe, one way or another. Perhaps now I can move on."

"Please do not speak of dying, Father. You are not an old man yet and have many years of life, with which to look forward."

"Who speaks of dying?" asked Mr Watson. "I wish to marry."

In the silence that followed, Mr Watson continued,

"Every being deserves to be happy, to find in another person – friendship, love and companionship. Every being deserves a second chance. I am an old romantic fool, you know this. Darling girls, I loved your mother. Truly, I did. But now I find I wish to share my life with another."

Emma at last spoke. "Whatever brings you comfort, we wish for you."

Elizabeth added, "How you fooled us with your suffering and lack of appetite. You were not dying, you were melancholic and forlorn. Who may we ask, is this most fortunate lady?"

Just then the door swung open and Mrs Ellingham, wide-eyed at seeing the group gathered around the bedside cried, "Am I too late?"

They turned to face her, Mr Watson uttering, *"But soft, what light through yonder window breaks?"*

Mr Howard ushered the girls out of the room, past a confused Mrs Ellingham, with "We will wait for you downstairs, Mrs Ellingham. Please be assured that all is well," leaving her to face a profession of love so effusive that even the great William Shakespeare himself would have blushed to have heard it.

CHAPTER TWENTY-EIGHT

As they reached the bottom of the stairs and Elizabeth made as if to open the door of the parlour, Mr Howard asked, "Miss Emma, would you do me the honour of taking a walk in the garden with me, if you do not find it too cold?"

Emma nodded and found Elizabeth placing her own shawl over her sister's shoulders before disappearing into the kitchen to tell Nanny to sit down for all the shocks she was about to receive.

They walked for some minutes in silence, more at ease now as a result of the spectacle they had just witnessed. Emma no longer feared being in his presence, for the humility of his behaviour indicated he held no ill will towards her.

"May we speak more of your plans to become a governess? I should like to help, if I can."

"Thank you. My aunt is offering her assistance," answered Emma, confused.

"I have access to a great many connections in several counties which you may find useful, if pursuing a career as a governess. They are at your disposal."

"Thank you," replied Emma, who was becoming distressed by his eagerness to help her find a post which would move her away from here – from him.

"Would it be a great disappointment for you to teach?"

"Momentarily, I believed it would be but not now, not once I became accustomed to the idea. Largely thanks to my experience at Wickstead, I have discovered that I love to teach. I fear, selfishly, that it does more good for me than for the pupil. My preference would be to teach those unfortunates who cannot afford an education. For now, however, it is a salaried post in a private home which I must seek. Soon I will not be needed here and I am confident that a good situation can be found."

"But you were forced to consider such an occupation. You would not have chosen it if ... if your brother had not threatened ..."

"No, I would not. But having been forced to consider it, I now rejoice that I am free to do so. I feel grateful to Robert for presenting me with the opportunity to become more me, not less me. He forced me into a corner where I believed I had no choices, but then I saw that there was a solution within my grasp. I could be of use by teaching and I could support myself. It has been a comfort to find that I could do *something* rather than sit and wait for something to be done unto me."

"I applaud you."

It appeared as if Mr Howard had more to say but he hesitated and into this silence Emma knew she must pour forth what was in her heart.

"I must commence seeking employment soon, Mr

Howard, and, therefore, must tell you something now, in the event that the opportunity does not arise again."

Emma continued to look forward as she walked, determining not to glance at her companion for fear it might prevent her saying what she must say.

"Mr Howard, I would not wish you to remember me as a dishonest person. I cannot bear to have you think ill of me. I have learned that my sister Penelope told you an untruth with regards to my actions and character. It was at Osborne Castle on the morning of the breakfast party. Believe me, I never broke your confidence and spoke of what you had told me. I did not betray your trust or friendship."

Mr Howard stopped and turned to face Emma who, with burning cheeks, was forced to face him too.

"I know, I really do know that now. And if I had not been the greatest simpleton alive, I would have believed it all along. But the testimony of a sister, a most likely confidante, stating that you saw me as a fool and shared my secrets, was impossible to ignore. I believed myself deceived by you. Then seeing how persistent Lord Osborne was and how everything pointed to the match –"

"I had never pointed to the match," interrupted Emma.

"No, you had not, and when I heard you had refused him, I realised I had been tricked. I should have come here immediately and begged forgiveness for my behaviour. Instead, I had another intention. Pardon my presumption, but I thought it best that, instead, I sanction the legal transfer of the new living at Branchfield so that when I approached you, I had more to offer, as well as a home secured for my sister. This required meeting with my lawyers in London. When I returned, all my hopes were crushed. I was embroiled in a scandal that would have you and everyone who cared for you shun me. I was not at liberty to act or publicly deny rumours – I had to wait for Musgrave's return to ensure that Lady Osborne's name was unsullied, but I was confident that he would do the honourable thing, thereby freeing me to act in my own interest again."

Such things to hear! Mr Howard had included her in his plans. He now indicated that they sit on the bench by placing his coat over it.

"Your letter and, especially, the map! Such a sign as this! If you only knew what it did to me and for me. It tortured me and gave me hope, in equal measure. You showed me kindness when it seemed I had not a friend in the world. Such kindness, from the very quarter I expected it least. I knew then what my feelings were and what I had lost. Emma, I have loved you from our first meeting – I have loved you with my whole being – nobody has been loved more. The walks here from Wickstead were the happiest times of my life. Even then I wanted to tell you what you meant to me but I could not. I hesitated. It was not that I felt too little, but that I felt too much."

Emma smiled broadly, delighting in all that he said and, afraid of any change in the direction of his declaration, nodded for him to continue.

"If you wish to tutor, if you wish to see more of the world, to move away and become a governess, I will support your decision and you will always have my friendship. But if you stay and wish to give instruction, as a clergyman's wife, I will endeavour to deserve and support you, in any way I can."

Emma, not wishing either of them to suffer for a moment longer, made it known in as brief a manner as her shortness of breath would allow her, that the second of the two options was her preference. They remained on the bench talking over the past and giddily planning for the future until, shivering at last, the cold forced them to continue their jubilation indoors.

That evening, nothing could spoil the celebratory mood around the dinner table, not even Margaret's scowl. If ever life presented a lesson to a young lady on the wickedness of gossip, the folly of pursuing an uninterested man and the uselessness of self-pity, it was then. Rather than learn and reflect on the part she had played in her own misery, however, Margaret threw her napkin onto the table and left for her room, remaining there for the entirety of the following day.

Mr Howard became a daily visitor to Stanton. During this time of courtship, he saw little of his own study and wrote some exceptionally short and lively sermons, to the confusion and delight of his congregation. A clergyman in love, they largely agreed, was a very good thing. One morning at Stanton, not long after their engagement was formed, Mr Howard was at leisure to explain to Emma in full, all that had happened in the weeks previous. She learned of the fate of Solomon Tomlinson.

"His damning open letter in the *London Gazette* had a two-fold effect. In the first instance, he was invited to join the most conservative evangelical church in London. They were excited to add such a fiery and unforgiving clergyman to their flock, or so he informed Lady Osborne when she ordered him to leave. So it was to this very welcoming group that he went."

"Poor London. I never thought it possible to feel sorry for a city." Emma laughed before asking, "And what, may I ask, is the second effect of his letter?"

"That Lady Osborne, who is in fact Mrs Oliver, the authoress, has been contacted by her publisher. He wished to inform her that a second printing is imminent due to the demand caused by the outraged letter."

Emma was shocked and delighted by this revelation and clapped her hands that Solomon Tomlinson's despicable letter had inadvertently contributed to the book's success. In addition, the thought that Lady Osborne, who had endured so much, was a novelist of renown, indicated a strength of spirit that Emma greatly admired.

"Do you believe that Lady Osborne and Tom Musgrave will be happy?" asked Emma.

"Undeniably! I am convinced of it."

"Perhaps this explains why he was careless with the hearts of others. It was to disguise where his true affections lay."

"Well, they delight in their situation, and, as your father said, every being deserves a second chance at love. She most certainly does."

Tired of talking of the happiness of another couple, Emma wished to turn the conversation back to her own.

"Did you, for a time, see me as your greatest enemy?"

"Yes, I fear, at first it was so. The hurt and humiliation I felt that day at Osborne Castle was severe and I found it impossible to bring my thoughts under control. If I had exercised more self-command and logic, I would have questioned the alleged betrayal sooner. But the pain was great and my mind clouded with doubts. For with Lord Osborne surrounding you and all others preferring him as your husband-to-be, my case appeared a hopeless one. Despite acknowledging you as an enemy, however, I could not rid you from my mind and I felt your presence everywhere. There was no refuge."

"I shall endeavour to be more mindful of your privacy in future. You may find sanctuary at your telescope. We shall be viewed as quite the peculiar pair – the clergyman astronomer and his tutor wife, but what of it, if we are happy."

"Now, with regards our large population of uneducated children – I spoke with Lady Osborne, as you requested, of your plans to establish a Sunday school. She is eager to meet with you to discuss it and wishes to offer her full patronage, if you will accept it. She is confident that other prominent members of Dorking society will likewise wish to offer support, including the Edwardses who have sought to tackle this issue for a long time."

"Then I truly cannot be happier than I am right now. So much happiness in so few days. How did I come to be so blessed?"

Mr Howard took Emma's hand.

"Because you are deserving, Emma. You are kind and it takes great courage to be kind. While others observe, judge or ignore, you act. For that you are rewarded and it is we who are blessed."

❖

And so it was, that on the same day as Solomon Tomlinson delivered his first sermon to a dumbfounded congregation in London, as Robert Watson retreated from a quarrelling wife and sister, as Lord Osborne and Miss Tomlinson rode out together to Box Hill – Mrs Ellingham and Mr Watson were wed. With the exception of Robert and Margaret, all their children were present at Stanton Chapel, joined by a large congregation of neighbours and friends.

Dr Richards, sitting in the second row, could hardly believe how young and lively Mr Watson appeared. It compelled him to lean forward in his seat and ask Dr Harding, in the row in front, whether he had ever observed such an alteration in a patient. Dr Harding, distracted momentarily by Nanny's yellow-ribboned bonnet, admitted he had not and wholeheartedly agreed that it was "absolutely" miraculous. Satisfied, Dr Richards leaned back in his pew, shaking his head and muttering, "Well, I never!" He determined, at that moment to himself and later that evening more loudly and with greater animation to any patron of the White Hart who would care to listen, never again to underestimate the harmful effects on the human anatomy of a disappointed heart or the benefits of a joyful one.

ACKNOWLEDGEMENTS

I send the following much love and gratitude:

My friends (old and new) and family (near and far) – for laughter, endless support, chats, hugs and tea. I may not always show it but I feel it deeply – I am blessed to know you. A special 'thank you' to Mark Jenkins, without whom I may not have sent any books out into the world.

The book club at Uncle Tom's Pub – the soundest bunch of people ever. If I turned up in my pyjamas they wouldn't bat an eyelid.

Those writers who have shown me kindness, camaraderie and made me feel welcome in their community. I have received shout-outs, emails, acknowledgements, pats on the back, and have made several new friends. A special mention goes to Donal Ryan who, when I turned up to his talk in November 2014, full of winter blues and baby blues, made me (and everyone in that room) believe they could write. And so I committed to trying – and here I am!

Bloggers, reviewers, librarians, book clubs, writer's retreats, festival organisers, Limerick Arts Office, The Arts Council of Ireland, Kazoo Independent Publishing Services, booksellers, readers and all those who treasure words, especially editor Sally Vince, without whose brilliance this book would be a quagmire of commas and long-windedness.

And finally to Jane Austen fans and societies all over the world (online and in the flesh), tea-drinkers, costumers, historical appreciators and period drama stage and screen enthusiasts, Austen friends (Natalie Jenner, Mark Brownlow, Nuala O'Connor, Eileen Collins and Karen Ievers) – what a joy-filled life this is, when we indulge in our passions!